Letters in Blood Book Two

LIZ LOVELOCK

DEDICATION

To my sister from another mister,
Jemma Brown.
Your friendship is one I'm truly glad to have
in my life.
You inspire me.
You push me.
You help me become better.
You're always there for me when I need you to kick my
butt into gear.
Thank you.

*"We all at certain times in our lives
find ourselves broken.
True strength is found in picking up the pieces."
~ Jill Pendley*

PROLOGUE

WHEN YOUR LIFE FLASHES BEFORE your eyes, what do you expect to see?

Joyful memories of your childhood.

The love of your life.

Friends who mean the world to you.

But when all you see is the man in the mask, it pushes you on. There are no memories of friends or family, just the desire and hope that you make it to the next day. That you survive.

My name is Elenore. My time came, and I was told to run. So that's what I did—I ran, even though the sticks and rocks dug farther into the cuts on my sliced feet. The pain only reminded me of what lurked behind.

Nothing would stop me.

Well, except maybe one thing.

A bullet.

1

CHAPTER ONE

Elenore

SEARING PAIN TEARS THROUGH MY upper thigh, as the echo of the gunshot rings out in the empty night. I collapse face first into the grass and rocks. More pain develops on my cheek as a stone pierces my skin. Not a sound escapes me, but I know I should be crying out. The burning in my leg is excruciating and causes my head to spin.

Get up, Elenore! Get up! My brain screams at me. I momentarily forgot where I was—now it all floods back.

Kidnapping.

Torture.

A memory of his voice yelling *"Run!"*

Being shot.

The man in the mask. I wonder if he's ever not killed one of his girls on the first shot. Why am I not dead?

Quickly, I pull my thoughts together and gather forward my willpower. I need to push into the forest line. That's where I was heading. I manage to pull myself up onto all fours, even though the agony is almost too much to bear.

My stomach heaves. Nothing but bile emerges. I push myself up onto wobbly legs. Glancing behind me, I see my captor with his head down, placed in his hands. What's going on with him? Who cares? I need to keep moving. Sluggishly, I begin moving at what feels like a turtle's pace, but each step bringing me closer to the edge spurs me on. My feet become quicker, even with one leg dragging, but somehow I manage to block out the pain in my thigh.

I meant what I said when I told my captor that I was stronger than he realized. I'll show him.

A stick snaps behind me. I spin and come face to face with those evil eyes. I fall backward.

"Where do you think *you're* going?" he hisses at me with such hate in the enunciated words. Swallowing hard, I remain quiet, my breath heavy. *"Answer me!"* he roars. It echoes out into the woods.

Sucking in a tight breath, my chest constricts,

4

only allowing a small intake of air. Clearing my throat, I swallow the hard lump in my throat. "You told me to run."

On my butt, I continue to use one leg to creep back ever-so-slowly. My captor turns away from me, looking around, then up at the sky. He appears torn. When his gaze falls back on me, he seems unsure, as if he's second guessing something.

Perhaps befriending him could save my life.

"Are you all right?" Sitting upright, I stop trying to move back. I can't see the gun in his hands, but I don't doubt that it's within his immediate reach.

At the sound of my voice, he pauses. I sense a battle waging within him as I feel my forehead crinkle with lines. If I was any other girl, I'd be dead by now. As much as I hate my past and the living hell I went through, it could be the one thing that saves me from this monster.

"Why would you ask me something like that?" Anger drips from his words.

Looking around, I'm still a reasonable distance from the forest, so I know I won't make it there if I try to run. Right now, it's stand and fight. I have so much hate welling inside me for this man, my captor, standing before me. He doesn't need to know that though—especially if I can twist it to work in my favor.

"Umm... you seem torn. Can't you let me go? I haven't seen your face. Please?" I beg, with the hope of changing his mind against killing me.

Without another word he storms toward me, grabbing my arm and yanking me to stand on my feet. His strength astounds me. His composure is fragile. Tonight didn't go as he planned, and I'm guessing it's all my fault. With his grip still attached to my upper arm, he stalks back toward the house. I stumble with each step taken and the agony shoots right through my leg causing me to stumble.

I try pulling my arm away from him. "Please let me go. I'll never tell a soul," I plead. With the thoughts of being locked up in that cell again, staring at the bloodstained walls, panic seizes my chest.

"No. You are mine." He yanks my arm not stopping—he's a man on a mission. What's the mission though? To cause me more pain?

I attempt to ground my feet, but the strain brings sharp pain to my leg, which gives way beneath me. A cry tears its way out of my throat, and I collapse on the ground once again. He releases his hold on me.

"Get up!" he roars, turning to face me, and pausing. He gives another shake of his head, then reaches for me again. As he gets closer, I bring my hand up, curled into a fist, and I strike him. When my hand connects with his face, I cry out again. My malnourished body isn't coping with the strain I'm placing on it.

I quickly attempt to scurry away, but he

pounces on me like a tiger on its prey.

"You bitch. You'll pay for that." There's promise in what he's said. I need a plan. I want to survive.

Hate for this man gives me the strength I need to get me through to the next day and the day after that. I'll never give up.

My captor pulls me to my feet once again.

I step closer. He steps back. As much as I want him to believe I care, I don't want to appear weak. With every bit of strength I can muster, I say, "Do your worst. Break me. I don't care. You're the weak one, not me."

CHAPTER TWO

Elenore

WHAT THE HELL IS THIS girl playing at? A mixture of anger, frustration, and confusion constricts my thoughts and actions. What is so different about this girl? Why did I miss my kill shot? And now because of that, here she stands before me, calling me weak. Deep down, I believe her; I am weak. I can't show her that, though. Shaking away my thoughts, rage causes my blood to pulse through my ears. My hand lashes out, striking her across her tear-stained face.

"Never speak to me like that again. I won't miss a second time."

"Go on then. Shoot me!" She shrugs my hand

off her and stands back with her arms wide open, waiting for me to pull out my gun and squeeze the trigger. She has a death wish. Yet, I can't bring myself to do it. Not now. A part of me wants to know more about her and what she's been through.

"I'll get you when you least expect it. I'll enjoy hearing your cries of pain—they feed and replenish me. That cell is going to be your home for a long time. Hope you like living in hell because you're about to have an extended stay." My laughter fills the silence of the night.

Taking her arm, I pull her along with me once again. She tries to tug away with every chance she gets. It comes to the point when I've had enough of the struggle and heave her over my shoulder.

She relaxes against me, which I find extremely odd. We enter the house. Looking around, I realize it's my own empty cell. We aren't so different, her and I.

Nothing in this house can be traced back to me. Always have a fallback, my father drilled into me, so I've had this place set up in case something ever went wrong. I never stay here—I have a different location, a home away from home, if you could call it that. I do love the outdoors here; it's something I miss when I'm away for work. Thank goodness technology has improved, and I can check in with cameras that are installed randomly around the property.

Once we're back in the cell, I drop her slack body onto the floor. It's then I realize something's wrong. Her eyes are closed. Her breathing short and very faint. She can't die like this. It's not the correct way. I race upstairs and out to my car where I keep a first-aid kit. Running back toward the house, I catch a glimpse of something out of place. Stopping, I refocus. It's her. She's running out into the night, toward the trees. Here I was thinking she's on her deathbed; instead, she's played me. Dropping the kit, I go after her. Even with a limp in her stride, she keeps going toward the forest.

I underestimated her.

That won't happen again.

My stride is longer and quicker, and it doesn't take long to catch up with her, tackling her to the ground.

"Get off of me, you creep!" She screams a mouthful of curses at me. Not only that, but she also manages to flip over and attempt to take off my mask. She pulls my head back, and an onslaught of blows are delivered to my neck. She lands one right on my Adam's apple. I'm left breathless for a moment, followed by a coughing fit. "Let me go!" she continues to scream.

"Shut it!" I say through clenched teeth. I stand huffing and puffing. I'm sick of putting up with her childish tantrums. I should have taken that second shot.

"Kill me then. I'm basically dead anyway, whether you keep me alive now or not. I'm sure you don't keep survivors. I may not be able to see your face, but your eyes speak to me in volumes."

Her words astound me. "You know nothing about me." I pull out the gun, which was tucked in my jeans, and aim it at her, flicking off the safety.

I watch her, amazed at her willpower. The nights before her were so still, until she came along and showed me such force. I wanted my songs of the night, the screams filling my ears. Now, this girl seems to have done something to me. I can't bring myself to do what needs to be done. She gets up and stands before me. I watch her struggle while her face scrunches up in pain. The whole episode bringing a slight curve to my lips. She flicks her messy brown hair away from her face and holds her arms out wide as if she's waiting for something.

"Shoot me. Get it over and done with. Stop making those who care about me suffer. Or do you want me to run again? I'm not sure I have much left in me, since you've starved me for the past week." She's not afraid. There's a fierceness to her I admire. She keeps telling me to kill her.

If my father were here, he wouldn't hesitate. I continue to hold my gun trained on her head. My finger dances with the trigger in disinclination. I observe her; she's basically skin and bones. Yes, I've starved her—it's what I've done with all of them. She sways slightly, as though she's a feather about to be swept away. Her tears are dried up, and her blue eyes pierce mine.

What did she say? *My eyes speak volumes…*

What can she see that I don't already know about myself? I know I'm a monster. I'm damaged. I'm a killer, and I don't know if I could ever change. Does she see the fight I have brewing within me? My monster, the killer inside me, wants to keep going. Then there's the other part of me. Though it's small, it's constantly there, wanting me to stop. With her standing before me basically giving herself over to my death sentence, the more humane part of me wants to take over. That's where the battle starts. I can't decide where my head and heart are.

I put the gun away. Her arms drop, then she sways again, and this time I catch her eyes rolling back into her head. *Damn!* Scooping her up before she falls onto the rocks again, I throw her over my shoulder. With a grunt and groan from her, I take her back inside collecting the kit on my way.

What am I going to do?

Let the battle of wills commence. It will either end in her survival or death.

CHAPTER THREE

Roman

AFTER A ROUGH AND LONG night, I stand outside Elenore's apartment door, a hot black coffee in my hand. Let's hope this wakes me up for the day. A couple of uniformed police officers had gone through her apartment the night she went missing. They'd been let in by the landlord. They reported back to Pierce and me, saying nothing appeared disturbed or out of place. I wanted to check it out myself.

My phone rings.

"Blackwood," I answer sharply.

"Where are you?" Pierce's angry tone slithers

through the line. He's wound up lately, so much more than usual.

"I'm standing at the door of Elenore's place. I wanted to check it out for myself."

"You do realize he usually keeps them a week then disposes of their bodies?"

Rolling my eyes, I respond, "Yes, I know that. I've been on these cases as long as you have. Perhaps we need to consider other options as well. What if we're wrong about who's got her?"

"I know and I'm always open to looking into other possibilities. You do realize today's the day something's supposed to turn up if it is the person we've been after?"

Anger burns inside me. Have I not stressed enough that this girl is actually special to me? If he were standing in front of me right now, I'd probably punch him.

"Pierce, don't remind me," I growl. "I'm hoping she's as strong as Suzie makes her out to be."

I hear a deep sigh on the end of the line. "I know. I'm sorry, man. These cases are really taking a toll on me."

"You and me both. How's this guy escaping us? His actions leave nothing for us to follow up. I keep asking myself the same damn questions every day." The community is stressed about the bodies of young girls that keep turning up. The police have no answers, except that we're doing our best. When he doesn't leave anything for us to trace, it makes me believe he's been doing this for much longer than we suspect.

"Me too. Let me know if you find anything new at Elenore's place."

I tell him I will, and we end our call. Taking another sip of my coffee, I pull the key Suzie gave me from my pocket.

"What do you think you're doing?" an angry, yet familiar voice yells. Spinning around, I come face to face with Lewis — the jerk.

"My job," I sneer, before turning my back and unlocking the door. I hear rushing footsteps behind me. Turning around, I press my hand on his chest. "You can't go in here. It's an ongoing investigation."

He pushes against my hand to get right up in my face. "Weren't you supposed to be with her that night? Yet, Elenore's not here anymore. Good job! Who knows where and when her body might show up... today, another day. Now, I've lost two friends." His voice cracks.

This is the kind of response I've seen a number of times in my career. Family and friends show anger because they don't want to deal with the worst possible outcome.

"I was running five minutes late. Cut me some slack. You don't think I'm torn up about this?" I shove him back, and Lewis stumbles slightly. His shoulders slump, in defeat.

He heaves a heavy sigh while running his

fingers through his already messy hair. "Sorry. I just can't lose her as well. Now, I think it's too late."

"I'm truly sorry, Lewis. I'm doing the best I can. Please let me and the rest of the team do their jobs." This is how I talk to someone who's lost someone special. Delivering bad news about loved ones is always so difficult, and it makes me nervous every time. This time isn't any easier. My emotions are all over the place, yet I have to keep them in check to be able to do my job to the best of my ability. I desperately want to find Elenore before it's too late.

"Sorry for being a jerk," Lewis says, before turning and walking away. His disheveled attire looks as if he hasn't slept or changed in days. His unshaven stubble, the food stains on his light blue button-up shirt, and the dark rings under his eyes are a clear indicator.

"Hey Lewis, how about you go get a shower and a change of clothes? You look terrible."

Lewis simply nods and keeps going. Poor guy.

Opening the door, the first thing I notice is it's so still. Elenore's scent of berries mixed with a hint of lavender slams into me like a freight train. I remember the first time I ran into her at the café, worry of running into me etched on her beautiful face, each crease on her forehead pulling the strings of my heart. Then she smiled and it was like the sun peaked through those storm clouds that were in full force outside.

Never has a girl like her, with her sassiness and not throwing herself at me, caused the type of stir I felt. When we met, I needed to know her straight away. What she liked. What she hated. What put that stellar smile on her face. She hadn't called me, and I had a feeling I'd not get the chance to know all those things about her until lo and behold, I stumbled into her workplace.

The taste of her sweetness, the softness of her lips have etched themselves into me. This woman is special. Elenore's a take-home-to-meet-your-parents kind of girl, and I will if I am given a chance.

My eyes take in her apartment. Everything's simple, but it's such a calming place. Turning, I shut the door with a faint click and immediately notice the quantity of locks on the door. They all lock from the inside, apart from the deadbolt that I unlocked.

Whoa! Is she afraid of something?

Perhaps it's who she is. Her childhood was awful and maybe it's how she feels safe. By locking herself in, she blocks out the outside world. Making sure she can't be hurt again, like she was when she was younger.

There's a small bookshelf filled with a limited collection of paperbacks. Some miniature photo frames sit in the front of a few books. Upon closer inspection, they're pictures of Suzie and her, some

of just her, and two of Elenore with Lewis and Rebecca. She appears to have a small network of close friends.

There's nothing out of place in Elenore's home — it's neat and tidy. You could assume that it's a model home, or that you're about to rent it fully furnished. Nothing appears unsettled in the living room or kitchen either.

Slowly, I move toward her bedroom. Usually, bedrooms hold people's deepest secrets, the ones we don't want anyone else to ever find. Stepping inside, I wish that these walls could talk. I'm sure they would give me something to go on. Something that would open up Elenore Burrows's world and let me in.

I check the bedside table with no luck. I know this is a part of the job, but why do I feel as if I'm prying? Opening the door to her walk-in closet, it's stocked with her beautiful, stylish shoes and fashionable clothes. I guess all this makes sense when you see where her place of employment is. You'd need to be on your A-game to work there. Seems to me like a dog-eat-dog world amongst the walls of *Forever You*.

I begin at one end of the closet and search behind the clothes. I check the floor beneath the hanging pieces of fabric. When I reach the middle, something doesn't look right with the wall. My heart leaps with excitement at the possibly of finding something.

After pulling out the items of clothing, I lay them on the bed carefully so I can gain a better view of the wall. It looks as if it's been repaired, like a piece of the wall was possibly removed and then fixed. Why would Elenore have something like this in her home? What secrets could she have hidden behind that wall? I apply pressure against the panel, and it creaks and cracks.

It's not very well hidden. Well, maybe for pathetic burglars, but not to the trained eye. To me, it stands out like a sore thumb. I pull out my pocket knife that's attached to my ankle and cut around the edges carefully. Plasterboard falls away. After a short time of careful cutting, I hook the blade behind the board, forcing it outward. Once I place it aside, I check what sits behind the wall with my torch, and I'm shocked. Behind the wall, covered in dust, is a stack of notebooks, journals maybe, and something else I never thought Elenore would own. A gun.

CHAPTER FOUR

Elenore
16 Years Old

CLASSES ARE VERY LONELY ONCE again, and the dirty looks I receive from my other classmates don't go unnoticed. I may as well have leprosy because they treat me as if I have some sort of terrible illness that people don't want to be around. At lunchtime I go back to the tree I usually sit and hide from the rest of my classmates, the place where I felt comfortable sitting all of last year. It is my sanctuary, away from the hustle and bustle, away from the glares that are becoming like shards of glass being stabbed into my heart. They dig deeper each time.

Taking a seat in my familiar spot, I pull out the brown paper bag Suzie had left for me this morning. There is a note. Recently, she's started writing inspirational letters to me. They help push me to be better and to want something more. Today's reads:

> *Elenore,*
>
> *You're much more than a child. You're a young woman with so much going for her. You'll be looked up to one day. It might be by your own kids, or maybe you'll change the lives of those around you. Be strong.*
>
> *Be you.*
>
> *Don't change for anyone.*
>
> *Suzie x*

"What ya doing?" A familiar slimy voice comes from behind me. I refold the cream colored paper with flowers on it, placing it in my bag and start eating my peanut butter and jelly sandwich. It is my favorite.

"Hi Dean," I respond politely, even though I don't want to be near him. For some reason, he makes me feel gross. He has bleached blond hair and blue eyes — he is the epitome of the school jock.

Dean takes a seat beside me. My inner alarm begins going off loudly, while the hair on the back of my neck prickles.

"Why aren't you inside?" He turns toward me, his hand reached out, and I flinch back.

"What are you doing?"

"Oh, come on, Elenore. I know you want me." I laugh at his statement.

His eyebrows draw together and his demeanor changes. Quickly, I clear my throat. "Look, Dean, I'm not sure what you think, but you have it all wrong. I'm not interested in you that way. I'm happy to be your friend, though."

In a flash, his hand has latched onto my hair, yanking it hard, pulling my face toward his.

"Ow! Let go of me!" I cry out, pain leeching into my scalp.

"You're nothing but trash and, I usually get what I want."

I cower away as he tries to plant his lips on mine, his free hand finding its way under my loose blouse, squeezing my breast. I shove him hard, but he doesn't budge, so I fall back with him on top of me. I came to school to escape my reality at home—now the bullying is happening in one place I thought was safe. A burning fire ignites. Something clicks into place, and I know I need to stand my ground or I'll be the one in trouble. Reaching down, I grab his dick and balls, twisting them with all my might. Dean's grip falters for a moment, so I take that brief relief and bring my knee up, connecting it where he is already hurting.

I've not seen a boy keel over and cry out so

quickly.

My breath grows heavy. I get up and collect my bag. "Stay away from me, you filthy pig. I want nothing to do with you ever again!" I point my finger at him. "I may be trash to you, but I'm worth something. I'm not some skank who'll let you willingly in my pants. Grow up." I turn and walk away leaving him in pain.

Looking toward the door, I spot Emma, her mouth hanging open. *Has she witnessed the whole thing?*

"He's all yours if you want him," I call to her before I walk out of the school, never to go back. I can't stand being in a place where everyone is so cruel to one another.

I'm worth so much more.

Elenore
Present Day - Day Nine

I OPEN MY EYES TO the darkness that surrounds me. It's night nine. Shifting slightly, I cry out in pain as a sharp ache shoots straight down my legs. Again, I'm reminded of the hell I'm in. Sitting up, my head spins, so I lean against the wall and wait for it to steady. My eyes fall on the bandage wrapped around my leg. It's probably the cleanest part of my entire body.

The scent of my dry vomit surrounds me, and then add in aromas of my bodily functions. Being in this cell is hell. What I wouldn't do right now for a shower.

It must be a full moon tonight. Tiny shards of light shine through the paper-covered window. The glow catches on a tray of food near the entrance of the cell, where I received my supper a few days ago. Pushing off the wall, I turn around and slide on my bottom toward the tray, since walking is out of the question for a while.

On the tray is a bottle of water, clean bandages, antiseptic cleaner—I guess for my wound—and a bowl of biscuits along with a cold what looks to be stew. Is he taking care of me now? He could easily let me die. I know attempting to escape again wasn't the smartest thing I've ever done, but I needed to try. I'll never go down without a fight.

I take a biscuit from the bowl and bite off some small pieces. Its saltiness tastes great.

I look down and notice I'm dressed in a simple white dress, it's like what he first put on me, but cleaner. My other one would have been covered in blood. Did he change me? Perhaps he has a conscience.

After a few moments, I observe an envelope on the tray, along with a pen.

"What's this?" I say. I take the small white envelope in my hand. Lifting the unsealed flap, I pull out the piece of paper from within. It's from him, my captor.

> *Elenore,*
> *You have a new death sentence.*
> *Only time will tell what's in store for you.*
> *Sincerely,*
> *Your Captor*

What the ever-loving hell is this? Here I was thinking he'd turned soft. Fear claws its way up my throat and tightens, restricting and cutting off my air supply. The throbbing in my leg tells me that I may not survive whatever it is he has in store for me. I'll not go down without a fight now.

"Do your worst, you pathetic man," I scream at the top of my lungs. I want him to hear me, to know that I'm not like his other captives. I'll never give up, not until my last breath is taken. I'll fight. The fighter I was when I was a teenager has come back with years more knowledge and so much more strength.

I sit and wait for him to show up with all his anger and rage. *Beat me or something*. Yet, there is nothing. Stillness fills the room like thick fog. He'll come when I least expect it, and no matter what, I'll be ready. I take the pen and turn the note over and begin penciling my own.

Dear Captor,

As I've said before… do your worst.

I've endured a lot in my life and put up with men like yourself. I do have to say, though, you're much more of a monster than them.

My parents were monsters, and they got what they deserved. So you see, I know a monster when I see one.

You'll get what's coming to you.

All in good time… all in good time.

Sincerely,

Elenore

CHAPTER FIVE

Roman

AFTER I CAME UPON THE gun and the journals, I took them back to the station, booking the gun in for ballistics and placing all the notebooks on my desk to go through. I go to Suzie's to question her about the findings. I give a sharp knock to the door once, and she opens it with tears in her eyes.

"We haven't found her," I quickly assure her, and a kind of relief washes over her features. Although this isn't the news she hoped for, it is news of hope, since we haven't found her body, which means she could be alive.

"Well, at least that's something, or you just haven't found her body. He could have hidden her so well that we don't find her," her words rush out.

I rest my hand on her shoulder giving her some comfort. "I know this is hard, Suzie. It's not usually this killer's modus operandi to keep the body hidden because he wants people to see his handiwork. Just remember it could be someone else still. We don't know."

She clutches a tissue in her hand and steps back, allowing me inside.

"I've come to talk to you about something I've discovered at Elenore's apartment."

"Take a seat. I'll get you a drink, then we can talk." She wanders off to the kitchen, and I can hear her pottering around, cupboards opening and shutting and the kettle boiling. I wonder how she'll take what I've found. We're still waiting for ballistics to come back on the gun, so we don't have much more information on that for now.

After a minute or two, Suzie comes back in with a tray of coffee and some home-baked cookies. They taste delicious—sugary goodness—simply melting in your mouth. She takes a seat across from me in one of her recliner chairs. It's the most worn chair in the entire living room.

"So tell me what's going on?" she begins.

I take a sip of the hot coffee. Suzie makes it just how I like it. "We found something at Elenore's apartment. Did you know she owned a gun?"

Suzie clutches her chest. Her eyes widen with shock. "What? No! She wouldn't. She would've told me if she was in trouble. We never kept secrets from each other."

I suspect Elenore definitely kept secrets from Suzie. "This gun in question was hidden behind a sealed part of the wall; she'd plastered over it. There was also about ten journals in there."

She pinches the bridge of her nose, then looks up at me pleadingly. "Can I see the journals? I used to buy her notebooks when she was a child and lived next door. Since she couldn't escape her reality, it gave her a chance to write down her emotions."

I nod. I haven't read any of the journals yet, but I plan to. "You can't see the journals right now, they're part of the investigation."

"Thank you. This entire situation is a mess. I want my girl home, safe and sound. Detective Blackwood… *please* bring her home."

Another rip to my heart. I may act all big macho man on the outside, but inside, this job really tears me apart. Especially now, watching Suzie.

"I'll do my best," I reply, because it's all I can do.

Back at the station, I sit at my desk with the pile of notebooks.

"What did her mother say?" Pierce says as he walks across and stands by my desk.

"She doesn't know anything about it," I

respond.

He folds his arms as he thinks for a moment. "Ballistics reports the gun's been used, but nothing shows up in the database as to who owned the gun previously or the bullets. There were a few fingerprints that, they've taken and are running them through the system now."

I nod. "I'm going to start reading some of these to get a feel for Elenore. Who she is. Maybe this isn't our serial killer? Perhaps it's a regular kidnapping." I run my fingers through my hair and sigh. "Remember her parents? They weren't the nicest of people. They dropped off the face of the earth. Maybe there's something in here…" I lay my hand on the dusty books, "that could possibly help us with their investigation as well."

Pierce scoffs. "Who cares about them? We have a missing girl here who might still be alive."

I sense his patience is wearing thin, as is my own. "I don't know, Pierce. I'm doing all I can, and if I have to sit here and read these over the next few days, I will. What the hell are you doing?" I never know what he's up to. Yes, we're partners, but there are times when I can't locate him. I'm always having to leave to find him. Terrible, I know, but I don't have the time to look for him when I'm trying to get things moving forward on the case.

"Out, getting some lunch… Be back soon." Without another word, he gets up and walks toward the door.

I stretch back in my chair and collect one of the journals, flipping it open. The handwriting is cursive and slightly messy, as you would imagine from any teenager. Reading the first sentence is like a knife to the gut.

Dear Diary,

Today I ended up in the hospital. My father used a blade on me. I have an open gash across my collarbone and arm. He completely went ballistic when he found out about Suzie and what she's been doing for me. When the doctor asked me about what happened, I lied. My father was standing there with his hard glare on me. I did what he wanted me to.

The day I came home early, I still had my nice shirt on display because I'd been so caught up in what Dean had tried to do to me that I'd forgotten to put my rags back on over my nice clothes.

He went crazy. I've never seen him like this before. I'm sure he would have let me bleed out if it wasn't for my mother screaming at him. That's the first time she's stood up for me, EVER. Maybe I'd be better off dead. It's not the first time I've thought about taking my own life, but the thought of actually doing it scares the hell out of me.

Now I have no friends again, I'm back to square one… a nobody. I don't plan on going back to school. That place is my second living hell. I'll figure something out.

It's now midnight as I write this. Tomorrow is my birthday, according to Suzie. I've never celebrated with my mom and dad, and I've always been too afraid to ask. I'll be seventeen.

I need to get my life on some sort of stable track. Perhaps I could leave this place and not come back.

But what about Suzie? I can't leave her; she's the only one who cares about me.

One day, my life will hopefully be better, and the two monsters who are my family will keel over and die, or something much, much worse. I kind of hope for the latter.

Love,

Elle

If she was seventeen when all this was happening to her, I hope she's strong enough for whatever this captor has in store for her now.

CHAPTER SIX

Elenore
Day Eleven

I HAVEN'T SEEN MY CAPTOR since he took the tray away while he thought I was sleeping last night. *I wonder if he read my note.*

I'm patiently waiting for what's going to come my way. I hate this man. What possesses a man to do this kind of stuff? The cuts he put on my feet four days ago seem to be healing all right, but they're warm to touch, so there's a possible infection now from running the other night. My bullet wound looks better than the cuts, amazingly enough. Thankfully, it was a through and through.

A loud bang sounds outside my little window, startling me upright.

My chest seizes… *He's here.*

I press my back up against the wall. My breathing becomes hard, as if there's a weight resting on my ribcage. Another bang sounds, only this time it's from within the house. My eyes stay trained on the bars of my cell, waiting for those black daggers to appear.

I don't have to wait long before they make their arrival. I follow each and every one of his movements. He walks backward and forward in front of the bars, watching me.

"What do you want?" I sneer at him, unable to help myself.

He stops and stands still. The silence is killing me right now. An eerie stillness lurks within these walls. What is he going to do? Is this it? My time to die?

I get up onto my throbbing feet. "What are you waiting for?" I scream at him.

He stands there and doesn't even flinch at the sudden screeching of my voice.

His hands dig into the pockets of his black pants. He only ever wears black attire. I fold my arms across my chest, panting at the effort it took for me to raise my voice. I watch his eyes crinkle at the sides, as if he's smiling. The mask covers his mouth, so I'm unsure.

Slowly, he pulls his hand from his pocket. Something's clutched in his fist. He releases a pin and throws it in my cell. I watch in horror as it rolls along the floor. Seconds later, a burst of smoke explodes from the device. The room fills, and when it hits me, I cry out in pain.

Tear gas! The stinging in my eyes feels as though acid has been poured over them. I begin coughing. Heaving. With each breath, it becomes harder and harder to breathe. I collapse to the floor, attempting to cover my face with clothing, but it's to no avail.

Gloved hands roughly grip my upper arm, pulling me out of the room once again and up the stairs. Each bruise he gave me last time is hit all over again, only this time he's not as rough. It still doesn't stop me from stumbling and coughing. My leg gives out beneath me, and I'm unable to get up again.

My eyes continue to burn with the unbearable pain. Squinting through slits, I feel the fresh air hit my exposed skin. I suck in a deep breath as the scent of pine fills my senses once again. Tears continue to pour down my cheeks, which makes the breeze colder on my skin.

Too bad I don't get to enjoy the moment any longer before I'm being dragged back to that familiar spot outside in the field. He throws me to the ground.

This is it. I'm going to die.

"Get up," he says with no emotion.

"I can't. My leg and feet hurt," I cry, and now I'm crying real tears—the kind that fear gives you, the kind I've cried before.

I hear a crunch then I'm heaved to my feet. I wobble when I'm placed down again, sure I'm going to topple over. I attempt to open my eyes without too much luck, because all I can see is blurry blobs.

"You're going to run again, and this time I won't miss."

"I can't."

"You can, *and you will*." He raises the volume in his voice at the end of the sentence.

"No."

I don't care. If this is my time to die, I'm going to stand my ground.

"If you want to kill me, do it while you look at my face, not while I'm running away with my back to you." My eyes remain shut and watering, but my other senses are heightened. I can hear his steady breathing, the shuffle of his feet, and even a bird or something swooping over the top of us.

"Run… *dammit!*" he shouts. I fall back with fright.

This time, I manage to get to my feet myself. "No!" I shout back as loudly as I can.

His heavy footsteps move toward to me, and I sense his closeness as goose bumps kiss my skin.

I try again to open my eyes. This time it's manageable, but my vision is still not good. He's a blurry blob, but now my captor's standing directly in front of me. The moonlight lighting his figure up. He's close enough for his breath to brush against my cheek. My heart hammers in my chest so fast I fear it might jump out of my throat and slam him in the face. Here's hoping anyway.

Seconds later, his knuckles smash against the side of my face. "Wipe that smirk off your face and *run!*"

My hand falls to my face that now pounds. This brings back so many memories for me. The father who disciplined me with the back and front of his hands pretty much every day of the week.

"This is nothing new. Keep going if it makes you feel better." I do one thing that I know will piss him off—I full-on grin. I wait for the second blow to come, but it doesn't. I can still hear his breathing before me, and I know I've stirred something inside him.

Within a moment, both his hands grip each side of my face. "You'll regret this." He breathes against my lips. Seconds later, something smashes against my lips, and only when he forces his tongue into my mouth do I realize he's kissing me.

I actually lean into him, pressing my body against his, kissing him back.

If this is how I survive, I'll do it.

CHAPTER SEVEN

Captor

HER LIPS ARE SOFT, LUSCIOUS, and inviting. Pushing into her mouth, I devour her unique flavor. The shocking part is… she presses her body against mine, causing a moan to escape my throat. Her hands come up to touch my face, but I stop her.

I don't know what's come over me. I shift her hands back to her sides, holding them there. Her body feels so good so close to mine. My hands want to wander around each and every one of her curves. *If my father saw me now…*

With that thought, I jerk back and shove her to the ground, pulling the mask over the lower part of my face again.

What have I done? My father would slash the ever-loving hell out of my back with his belt if he saw this.

"I'm sorry," she murmurs, cowering away and not looking up at me.

My hard stare falls upon her. Stepping into her space I tower over her. I whip my hand back. Leaning over, I strike her across the face. Her soft flesh stings against the palm of my hand. The joy it once held for me is still there, but not as strong. She cries out in pain, but she's not distraught like other girls would be.

What am I saying? By now, if it were any other girl she'd be dead in a ditch, and I'd be relishing in the chase, the escape, being able to live a life where no one knows who I am.

"This is all your fault," I bellow out into the night air. I'm not sure if my outburst is aimed at her, me, or my father.

Her small voice starts to speak, pulling me back to her. "Please let me go."

I let her words mull in my head for a few seconds before I draw my hand back and hit her again, this time harder. "Get up!" I growl.

Without a word, she slowly pulls herself off the ground. She's still coughing from the tear gas I threw into her cell. Once she's upright, she stands before me with her arms wide open, ready and waiting for what though? For me to kill her or kiss her again? This girl has such strength. I've never witnessed this in any of the girls before her. A part of me wants to find out more about her, but the other part, the family tradition-focused part, wants me to inflict more pain upon her.

"Do it," she says, her voice barely a whisper. She takes a hesitant step closer and continues until she sways in front of me. She squints, and I catch the glistening of tears on her cheeks. These aren't tears of fear or sadness — they're from what I inflicted on her. Her body moves closer, and I fight the urge that burns within me to take her, all of her, and have my way with her.

"Do it, kill me," she whispers again.

I shove her back. She falls again. The struggle raging inside my head continues.

Why can't I pull the trigger?

Squeezing my eyes shut, I rub my forehead. My feet move as I pace the rocky ground. I have no choice. I have to be true to my family, my roots, my living essence. I retrieve the gun tucked in the back of my jeans.

"You have till the count of twenty to run. So get up." The roughness I usually hold in my voice now falters. Quickly clearing my throat, I flick the mental switch, the one that makes me inhumane.

"One, two, three, four…" I count, and again, she manages to pull herself up. This time she stands there watching me, a puzzled look on her porcelain face. The dirt which smears over it is my doing, and I actually hate myself because of it. I want to see her face clear and bright once again.

"Five, six, seven, eight... You need to run," I push.

With my gun in one hand, I take the pocket knife from my jacket. When I look up, she has her back to me and is walking.

Seriously!

Walking!

What game is she playing at?

In a rage, I take two large strides and push the blade I'm holding down her back, cutting through the thin material of her dress and slicing into her unmarred skin. She screams. My song of the night. It's back. My heart races with pleasure. My stomach twists with excitement. This is what I need.

The more pain I inflict, the better I deal with my mess of emotions.

I remember when my father delivered my first girl to me. I was eighteen. It was like an induction into the family tradition. I remember her blood-stained platinum blonde hair, her eyes bloodshot from crying and begging. My father had her lying on the exact same gurney that I use today. The words he spoke to me ring loud and clear in my mind every time I have a new girl. *"Inflict pain, Son. Once you do it, it'll be the only kind of pleasure that really makes you happy."*

I'd taken the blade from his hand; mine had

been shaking. I'd been conditioned for this family tradition, as my father and grandfather called it. Enrolled in every form of self-defense class, taught by my father how to handle the girls. He was my idol, or so I'd thought.

That day, I took the blade for the very first time and sliced her feet. Her screams still haunt me every night—no one else's but hers. She was my first. Blood had slowly trickled from the cuts, and by the time I'd finished, the girl had passed out. I actually threw up after that.

"Don't worry, Son. I was sick my first time as well. It gets easier, and you'll get more enjoyment out of it each time."

He was right. It has become easier, but why is this girl affecting me so much now? Her limp body now lies unmoving on the filthy ground.

I should finish her. But something holds me back.

"Get up!" I kick her in the ribs and hear a huff of a breath escape from her mouth.

This girl, Elenore, raises her head, looking at me with pleading eyes. Her head falls, and again, she ever-so-slowly gets up. I could run a lap around this paddock before she's even finished rising. As she stands, her rag falls from her body. I suck in my lip and bite it, restraining myself from reaching out and touching her flesh. Caressing it.

Hell! I'm done for.

Again, she turns and begins walking away from

me. I watch streaks of blood trickle down her back, forming rivulets and soaking into the edge of her panties. Guilt grips my gut, and I can't take this battle within me anymore.

I raise my gun. Taking aim.

This is it.

This is her death… *finally*.

CHAPTER EIGHT

Elenore

THE PAIN BURNS DOWN MY spine. I thought something within him was changing. Now I understand he has something he's fighting against—himself. He's his own worst enemy. Inflicting pain must help him feel better about something. I only wish I knew what.

Is he afraid to hold some feelings for me?

While I walk, the warmth of the blood on my back doesn't go unnoticed. As much as it hurts, I don't want him to see me weak. The tears want to fall, but I won't allow them to. My eyes already sting from the tear gas. Early on in my life, I learnt not to show weakness—it only makes you more of a target for those who seek enjoyment from your pain. I learned to stand firm in the face of danger. It took me a long time to find my backbone, but when I did, I held strong, and I'm not letting that go.

A lightheaded sensation settles behind my eyes. Bright spots begin to dance in my vision, but I push on. I'll keep walking until he pulls that trigger as he so desperately wants to. Behind me, I hear it click.

And wait.

And wait.

Inch by inch, I keep walking.

"Just do it already," I whisper to myself. I know he can't hear me, though. Even the sharp rocks and sticks that have been digging into my now open wounds haven't bothered me. I know my strength. I'll keep going until my last breath.

BANG!

The gun rings out into the night, but nothing new hurts. Spinning around, I'm faced with those eyes. They'll haunt me forever. Ever so gently, he scoops me up in his arms. If I weren't in pain, I'd probably kick and scream, fighting him each step of the way but instead, I collapse into his embrace willingly.

I need to play my cards right, though.

"What are you doing to me?" he whispers.

There's something I notice about his voice—it's

familiar.

No. I don't believe anyone I know would cause me this much pain. Well, except for my own parents. My mind must be playing tricks on me.

I respond to him drowsily, "I don't know what you mean. I need to sleep now."

"No, you can't." His panicked voice startles me awake, only for a brief moment. My eyelids feel like lead.

"I can't keep my eyes open."

"If you shut them you might not wake up. Is that want you want?"

"No, it's what you want, though. Me gone."

With those final words, blackness takes over, all pain floating away.

Brightness surrounds me.

Am I dead? Is this what Heaven looks like?

I'm in a floating cloud with a white haziness encircling me.

"Hello, beautiful girl." That angelic voice embraces me like a warm hug.

My spine tingles. "Who's there?" I call out, unable to see anyone in the thick white fogginess.

When I turn around, I'm confronted with a foggy memory of some sort. It flashes up on the clouds like a projector. A young woman, her dark hair high up in a messy bun. Her arms are

outstretched waiting for something when a little chubby little girl bounces into her arms.

This looks familiar. I remember something like this.

The bright green grass and swing-set are in the yard as the young woman chases the little girl around and they giggle with each other.

I'm sure if my parents ever played with me like this I'd remember. I only remember the bad with them—every cut, every bruise they laid upon my skin.

I shiver simply thinking about it. The scars are permanent reminders of what I never wanted to happen to me again. Yet, here I am, floating in what looks like the in between, but I'm not sure. One thing I do know is that I'll be waking up in that stale-smelling cell again.

"Mommy's coming to get you," the young woman calls to the little one, who lets the happiest squeal go before running and hiding behind a yellow rose bush.

"Where's my princess?" the mother calls after her child.

I watch this play out before me, and before it happens, I already know the little girl is going to get a thorn in her hand. Seconds later, a cry of terror screams out. The mother's face turns to one of panic. She follows the cries and finds her little girl on the ground nursing her hand, blood dripping from it.

"Oh baby, Mommy's got you. Let's go get that

cleaned up. Did the rose bush bite you?" The way she talks to her toddler soothes her—actually, it soothes me. The toddler nods and continues to cry. I watch the mother take her inside and clean her up, dressing the wound and placing a kiss on her daughter's temple. I recall a very thin memory like the one playing out before me.

My gaze fall to my hands, and there's blood all over them. Tears prick my eyes when I see the end of thorns poking out from my fingertips. It doesn't hurt, but the blood keeps coming. I frantically try pulling out the thorns, only for more to grow on my skin on a different part of my body. My stomach. My arms. My feet. My body is a thorny pincushion with red liquid seeping from each puncture.

What's happening? Dread fills every inch of me.

A black fog takes over the beautiful white space.

"No! Please no," I call out, pure fear in my words. Not knowing what's going to happen is my greatest fear. I stand stock-still as the thorns invade every part of me.

Why aren't they hurting me?

My blood pours from the thorny holes in my skin.

What's happening? A terrifying scream bellows from my chest. Why am I not waking up?

I fall to the grass beneath me. "What is this place? Hell?" I call again while waiting for someone to answer me. Please answer me. The heaviness in my chest fills my entire body until breathing becomes the greatest challenge. When I lift my head toward where I last saw the mother looking after her child, she's gone, and those black eyes are back, pouring their hatred for me into my body.

CHAPTER NINE

Roman

Dear Diary,

Today I spent my day locked in the dark room. Since I'm no longer at school, the monsters punish me more. Why am I being punished? Did I do something wrong in another life?

I sat in that hell hole, listening to a tap drip all day. I had my stash of food and water, which was my lifesaver because they never brought me anything to eat. I'm surprised my stomach and body still function, and that I'm not shutting down after the way I've been treated.

I can't wait to get out of this house. As soon as I turn eighteen, I'm gone. I could leave now, but where would I go?

Last night, Suzie left me a new notebook, pen and some sweets in our secret spot. It fits my lunches in there perfectly, and anything else she gets me. Since our house is low-set, I climb out my window when I know the monsters are in bed. Sometimes, Suzie is up waiting for me, and she'll give me a plate of food to eat. Her roasts are the best; her homemade gravy is mouthwatering.

I've decided to not dwell too much on the hell I'm living in, but to look to my future. I want a bright one, one where I'm in charge of everything. I can't wait to get a job and make my own money. I could look for a job now, but maybe that's not a good idea when I'd be turning up with bruises or not at all when I'm locked away like I am today.

The monsters weren't happy that I wasn't going to school anymore. Now I'm being punished for every little thing. Hell, I was brushing my hair the other morning, and because a few strands of my hair were on the floor, I received smacks around the face. I now sport a black eye to go with my malnourishment.

I WILL become something worthwhile and be happy. Those are my life goals.

That's all for tonight.

Love,

Elle

Each entry I read makes me angrier. Heck, I snapped at the worker delivering office mail before because he interrupted me. I have to get out of this office for a while.

Elenore was sixteen when all this was happening to her. No sixteen-year-old should be put through this kind of childhood.

"Pierce, did we get bloodwork back on the drops that were found from Elenore's last known location?" I call to him before I head out the door.

He grabs a file and flips it open. *How did I not know this had come in?* "I got it about five minutes ago, and haven't had a chance to look over it just yet." He peruses the paperwork before him, while I stand by, twiddling my thumbs. His brow furrows as if he does not understand what's written in front of him.

"What's wrong?" I ask.

"Well, the blood matches that of a missing person from twelve years ago, Rose Billings. But that can't be possible. Right?"

He looks up at me, the puzzled look still plastered on his face. What he's saying is not what I expected. *This gets weirder and weirder.*

"Are you sure they didn't mix up the bloodwork?" I need to know. Elenore has been gone for twelve days with no word and no body.

"I'll get them to run it again." He picks up his phone. "Wait... who reported her missing?"

Pierce types a few things on his keyboard. "Oh my…" He pauses, his eyes scanning what's in front of him.

Screw this. I read over his shoulder, and my mouth drops open. Elenore or Rose's missing reports were lodged by one of the wealthiest families in New York. They own a large investment company—TAB Investments. The owners are Tabatha and Andrew Billings. "Damn. Just what we need," I mutter under my breath. "Don't let this get out right now. I'll talk to the captain, and I want to talk to her adoptive mother, Suzie, again. Keep this under wraps," I hiss at him.

Back at Suzie's, I sit in the now familiar living room. I don't hold back on account of her feelings anymore, as I seek answers to Elenore's life.

"So Suzie, can you tell me… were the Smiths your neighbors for a long time?" I start.

Suzie ponders for a moment, sipping her tea. "I've been here since I was married, so a number of years. I remember when they moved in they had Elenore with them. She was a child." My chest tightens as she continues to speak. "The poor girl was like a zombie, walked around dazed and continually crying to go home."

My suspicions were beginning to become a reality. "Crying to go home?" I question.

She nods. "I just assumed she wasn't happy that

they moved here. She already had bruises on her arms and large dark rings under her eyes. The poor dear."

This isn't what I wanted to hear. I've read four of Elenore's journals over the last few days. Each entry describes some kind of hell she went through. I wish I could go back in time and take her from that place. A part of me wants to yell at Suzie and ask why she couldn't have done more for the girl. More should have been done for her.

"Damn," I curse under my breath.

"What's wrong?"

Lifting my head, I come face to face with her pleading stare. Suzie has unshed tears in her eyes.

"Well…" I pause, unsure how to tell her. As my mother would say, I need to rip the Band-Aid off and expose the wound. "Today we got the bloodwork back… There were drops of blood at the kidnapping scene. We ran them through the system, hoping to pinpoint a connection with her parents. Instead, it came back with a missing person's report, which matched to a girl who was reported missing about twelve years ago."

Suzie sucks in a hard breath, cursing quietly. Her trembling hands cover her mouth, her tears now falling down her cheeks. "Wh… How did this go unnoticed? Police had been to their place when she was little, too. How did they not recognize her?"

Questions keep coming, ones I can't answer.

I will be looking further into these reports that's for damn sure.

Placing my hand on her knee for some sort of comfort, I tell her, "I'm not sure, but I promise you that I'll be getting to the bottom of it. Your questions will not go unanswered. I guarantee you."

"I could have helped her, and gotten her back to her family." She cries, her sobs becoming harder and harder.

"Do you have anyone we can call?"

She shakes her head. "No, I'll be all right. My husband passed away, and we never had children. I have a sister, but she's a few hours away. I'll be fine," Suzie assures me as I watch the small tears slide down her face. She catches them with her tissue.

I'm saddened for her.

Standing up, I place the cup I'd been holding back on her tray. "I'm so sorry, Suzie."

She stands, placing her arms around me and giving me a hug, and I return it. She needs someone. That person is usually Elenore, but I'll take her place for now.

"I have to go, but I promise I'll be back and when I do I'll bring answers with me."

She nods while wiping her eyes. "Promise me another thing?"

"Sure."

"If you happen to find those monsters who called themselves her parents, make sure they're in a ditch somewhere. But if not, I'd sure like them to be." I catch the pure rage that flames in her glassy eyes.

"Between you and me, Suzie, they won't live to see another day of sunlight."

CHAPTER TEN

Elenore
Day Thirteen

"URGH…" I GRUMBLE. I'VE COME back to reality. Every part of me pulses with continuous throbs of excruciating pain. My eyes aren't willing to open, and they still burn.

I'm not alone. Whoever is there isn't making any noise, but I can hear their breathing.

"Welcome back." The chilling voice sends a spike of dread right through me, from the top of my head down to the tips of my toes.

I want to scoot away from him. I would have thought he'd leave me in the paddock to die a slow

death. Then I recall him telling me not to close my eyes. Perhaps I was dreaming that. Did I also dream up the kiss?

Something wet is across my eyes, and I flinch away from the touch. "Don't touch me," I hiss.

I hear a huff of breath. "It's only a wet washcloth."

"Why do you care? Don't you want to put a bullet in my back?" I bite back. My throat scratches, which brings on a coughing fit. Seconds later, a bottle is at my lips, and I turn my head away.

"It's water, you stupid girl." Annoyance is etched in his voice.

"For all I know it's poison... just like you." I desperately want that drink, but I'd rather be back in my cell drinking the bottled water or even the water from the sprinkler on the ceiling. Not receiving care from this villain.

"If you were anyone else, you'd be dead by now. Be grateful." His words echo around the room.

"Dead!" I make an attempt to sit up, but I'm pushed back down. "You're gutless that's what you are." I laugh and pull the cloth away from my eyes. I attempt to open them again, and this time I succeed. Things around me are still blurry, but I don't miss the tall, sculpted figure standing beside the gurney.

I'm back in the room of pain. Last time I was

here, he sliced my feet.

"You'll learn your place soon enough." After he says those words, I feel a sharp prick to my arm. I'm coherent enough to sense something gliding down my face gently, with care.

Is it him? I lean into what I assume is his touch, as I'm claimed by the white fogginess once again.

Elenore
17 Years Old

GIVE UP…

Those words sound so tantalizing. Give up this life, this family, and my continuous struggle to survive. No person on this earth should have to live like this.

A trip to the hospital happened today. My father keeps with his weapon of choice—the knife. Since using it on me last time, he's taken to it more regularly.

What lies are they telling the hospital? It isn't the first time I've been there. The desire to end it all is so strong. My body's tired of always trying fight. My mind's exhausted from constantly being on alert. I am sick of fighting,

After the same doctor had patched me up, he watched me. It looked like he wanted to say

something, but his questions never left his mouth.

My mother, at no time, left the room.

When I finally caught the eye of the doctor, his eyes didn't leave mine, and he mouthed to me "*Are you okay?*"

I shrugged. I wanted to cry out for help. I wanted to be taken away from these monsters. They were seasoned liars. Yes, we'd had the police called to our home, and when that happened, they had me doing the dishes and told me never to turn around. Even when the officers asked to see my face, I had to assure them I was okay. It hurt when they walked away.

I always did as I was told. I knew what was good for me.

On our drive home, I had *the lecture* from mother. "You brought this on yourself. Everything that happens to you is *your* fault." She paused and looked over at me while we waited at a red light, I felt her eyes on me burning like lasers. I couldn't bring myself to look at her, so I kept my head leaning against the window. I stared out of the windscreen. I watched all these cars around me. They had a mixture of families, couples, young kids, who had just gotten their licenses. And the one thing that stood out to me was… they all seemed happy. *Why can't I be happy?*

I was sure families fought, and parents spanked their kids when they needed it, but why was I living in this hell? Was God punishing me for something I'd done?

I watched the people walking the streets, chatting with their friends. I desperately wanted that. If only I could get away from these monsters.

Since getting home from the hospital, I've been locked in the dark room for who knows how long. I am sure it isn't still the same day, though. I hadn't even had time to replenish my stash of food from my last visit in here. The dirt floor seems to collect water when it rains, and it's been raining on and off since we arrived back from the hospital. Now, I am sitting in slushy brown mud.

At least I've learned quickly to fend for myself and to manage my survival.

Although, right now, I want to give up. Throw it all away, my life—if you could even call this a life.

End it all. To take away my pain and loneliness.

Next chance I get I am so done.

I can't take any more.

CHAPTER ELEVEN

Captor

I WATCH HER BODY GO limp after I inject her with a fast-working sedative. This girl will be my undoing. I have something new stirring within my veins, and I'm not sure what it is.

I want to know more about her, but I can't show weakness, or she could use that against me.

I wonder if I could get her to divulge stuff to me if I write her another letter. As she leans into my hand while I trace the silkiness of her skin, desire sparks inside of me.

I'm not sure I can kill this girl.

She has warped my sense of punishment, and I

only want to make her feel good now. The memory of her lips on mine twists my stomach in a good way. I want more. I want my hands to claim her body as my own. Her fighting has shown me that no matter what's thrown at you, you can change your path.

I leave her lying in the operation room. Stepping out, I'm in the basement. Battle wages within me... Do I put her back in her cell or place her in the upstairs room?

I shake my head furiously. What the hell am I thinking? This isn't the family way. Turning around to where she lies on the gurney, I scoop her up in my arms and take her now limp body back to her cell. Gently, I place her down on the tattered mess on the floor. I screw my face up at the smell that wafts through my mask. Because none of the other girls have lived this long, I've never had to deal with continuously emptying the bathroom bucket. But because I've kept her longer, I'm forced to do it.

My fingers remove the hair that has fallen over her beautiful eyes. *What am I going to do?*

My head continues the battle it's been having with itself since I first decided to let her live. Turning around, I leave the filthy room. I take one last glance at the beauty who lies there looking peaceful. Like she doesn't have a care in the world. That all changed the moment I entered her life.

Slowly, I make my way up the stairs leading

back to the house area. I set to work getting her a tray of food. Another bowl of beef stew, a bottle of water, and this time I'm going to add something sweet. I find a box of Twinkies and place two on the tray. Not the most appetizing meal, but it's not meant to be. Even though she should already be dead and her family in mourning, I need to figure out what made me miss that shot I've made a number of times. As a last thought, I add some bandages and antiseptic for her wounds.

I would like her to trust me. I need her to tell me why she fights so hard, and have her open up to me. I take some paper and a pen, placing it neatly on the tray.

I have a plan to get her to tell me more. It all starts now.

CHAPTER TWELVE

Elenore
Day Fourteen

ANOTHER DAY ALONE IN MY cage. The sun shines brightly outside and every now and then I'll hear the singing of birds. *I wonder how far out of the city I am.* My eyes fall on my dirty dress. This is the second one I've been dressed in, but it too is now covered in blood. My own.

What I wouldn't give to walk around outside — to feel the heat of the sun's rays touching my skin. My captor has placed cleaning items for the cuts on my feet by the little door which the tray of food comes through, which surprises me. When I apply the alcohol cleaner, a hiss escapes my lips. The sting shoots pain up my leg. I keep going, putting up with each stab of pain until they're clear of grime.

With my feet now cleaned and dressed, I dig into my usual menu. I gag at the thought of eating another spoonful of the brown mush.

Just to piss him off, I throw it at the wall outside of the bars. Suck on that! Perhaps he'll clean out this filthy cell as well.

I've been living in this filth for, I think, fourteen days now. Since he's been feeding me more often, I have much more strength than I did at the start. I'm pretty sure that's not what he did with his other girls—basically, he starved them so they couldn't fight back. *What makes me so different?*

The pen and paper don't go unnoticed either. What? Does he want another hateful letter? *I'll be happy to give him that*, I think, as I smile to myself.

Today, there's also something sweet on the tray—Twinkies. I've actually never had them before. Suzie has always been a home baker, and of course, my parents never allowed me them. They'd have seen them as a treat, which was something I was never allowed. Unwrapping it, I put it up to my nose, taking in the smell. It smells like a sweet cake. My mouth waters, and my taste buds tingle. I sink my teeth into it, and a groan escapes me straight away. It tastes so much better than I'd thought it would. A million times better than the mush I've been eating. I inhale the

Twinkies so quickly that I get a small pain in my stomach. My damn stomach has been playing up since I've been starved, cramps even invading my sleep. Nothing I do gets rid of them.

Perhaps, I'll throw that out at him, I think with a giggle.

I eye the bucket. The idea mulls around in my head. It sure would get his attention.

I glance up at the camera in the corner of the room. "How about a clean room? That wouldn't go astray," I shout, hoping that he's most likely listening and watching. "And how about something to settle my stomach that you've stuffed up? While you're at it… get me something other than this sickening mush. And I want more sweets," I yell, placing my orders to the camera. Let's see what he comes back with.

Leaning against the wall, I take the pen and paper, pondering over what I should write. I've spent most of my life writing. Keeping a diary when I was younger really helped me push through all those times that were a challenge. I'm not sure even what's written in most of them now, but there's one that sticks in my mind so clearly that it haunts me. I'm glad no one will ever read them. I put them away in a safe place.

Swirling the pencil in between my fingers, it hits me.

Dear Captor,

What do you see when you look in the mirror?

When I look into those black eyes, I see darkness and hate, especially toward me. Yet, I feel there's a story behind them. You're torn about something. My guess would be me, but maybe something else as well.

I don't care what you do to me. I'll never give up.

So good luck.

Sincerely,

Elenore

I fold the paper up and slip it back on the tray. Slowly, I crawl back to bed, collapsing onto it. I miss my home. I want my bed, much better food, and of course, to see Suzie. She must be going crazy. I can imagine her annoying the police, trying to get some answers.

Are they going to search my apartment? My stomach plummets. What if they find my diaries and the gun? I hope I've managed to make the fixed wall look like it was already there. When and if I get out of here I will destroy those books, and that gun will be gone as well. I'm not even sure why I kept them. I guess they were a part of me, and I needed a reminder of who I didn't want to be again.

Closing my eyes, I think of the lady in my dreams. In the first one she was blurry, but in the second one, something about her seemed so familiar. Hell, she even looked very similar to me, but she wasn't my mother. No, my mother was never kind like that. I don't think I ever witnessed a smile as bright as the sun like the lady in my dream had as she watched over and played with her child. Why hadn't my own mother treated me like that?

Why have these dreams never happened before? Perhaps the drama of what I've been going through has sparked something that's been lost in my memory, blocked. I wish I could get more answers. I need to know what this all means.

CHAPTER THIRTEEN

Roman

WALKING INTO THE STATION, READY to start the day, I feel brighter. It's amazing what an actual night's sleep will do for you. I scan the office and see that Pierce isn't here even though he should be.

Turning to the closest officer, I ask, "Where's Pierce?"

He shrugs and keeps walking.

"Great help there, buddy," I mutter under my breath.

Pulling my cell from my coat pocket, I hit Pierce's name. It takes him longer than usual to answer. "What?" he grumbles.

"Good morning to you, too. Where the hell are you?" I bark, frustrated at him for not being here since we have a meeting with Elenore's biological parents this morning, and here he is, being a lazy ass and sounding half asleep.

"Oh, come off it, Blackwood, you've been slacking lately as well. I slept in, cut me some slack."

I've been slacking? If steam could come from my ears, I'm sure it would be pouring out by now. This guy is starting to really get on my nerves. Yes, he's good at his job, but damn, some days I want to strangle him.

"What the hell are you on about? I've been working harder than you." I flop down into my desk chair. "Did you get any further information from ballistics on the gun yet?" I ask.

"Whatever, man. I'm up now, and I'll be in shortly. As for ballistics, they should be coming in today. They found some fingerprints in the system that match what they found on the gun. There was more than one set."

I release a breath. "Whose were they?" I already have a feeling about who one of those sets belong to, but the big question is, what or who did she use it on? The chamber was missing four bullets.

"They haven't come back with all the details yet. I'll talk to you when I get in." He ends the call, and I'm left staring at my computer screen. This entire case is a mess; there's more to this girl than meets the eye. Reading her diaries has given me an insight into Elenore's past.

I'm a little hesitant to read the next entry. Elenore's been through so much, and I'm scared to see what else she endured. With reluctance, I pick up the off-colored book and open to the next entry.

Dear Diary,

Today I snuck out of the house to go to the library. I was in desperate need of escapism. At the library, I hide away in the corner from the world, with my nose deep in a new adventure of a book of my choosing. The smell of paperbacks are relaxing.

While I was there, I got a visit from the dropkick Dean. Let's just say he wasn't happy to see me. I'd made a fool of him in front of some students, and now I've ruined him, as he told me today. He informed me that I'm worthless and a no one.

If I didn't already know that then I'd be hurt. I've been told these things on a daily basis, so today when Dean said them to me I smiled at him. I bared my teeth, and gave a very generous grin. I told him thanks for the compliment. The look on his face was somewhat of a shock.

He asked why I didn't let things get to me. I told him that some people already live in Hell, so it doesn't much matter what others do or say because their everyday is so much worse.

He sat down beside me and actually said sorry for being such a dick. Of course, I accepted his apology. I try not to hold grudges against people. It's not who I am.

Dean stayed at the library with me for a little while. He actually chatted with me and wanted to get to know me as someone other than the weird girl. It was nice getting to know him on a different level.

Sometimes I wonder if I even belong to my parents. I don't think I look like them. I mean, my mother has blonde hair and, well, my father is bald, so I don't know where I get my dark hair from. I don't mention it because I remember asking when I was younger and they told me to never ask again and gave me a smack for good measure.

I always wonder why we never have family or friends over. As I've gotten older, I've asked, but receive no answer, just more bruises. I guess one day I'll find out the truth.

I've holed myself up in my room tonight with a book I 'borrowed' from the library. I don't have a library card, and with no I.D. I've not been able to get one, so I put a book in my backpack and 'borrowed' it, then I'll return it when I get a chance to go back. Not the most honest way, but I need to live in my books and not my reality.

Tonight, my parents didn't actually speak to or acknowledge me. They seem to be caught up in something serious. There were harsh whispers between them, and they were giving me sidelong glances. I made a quick escape before I landed myself in trouble.

Well, that's all for me tonight. More tomorrow, hopefully.

Love,

Elle

Leaning back in my chair, I'm relieved that there was no hard stuff in this entry like the others I've read. I've not read every single one, but I have the majority. Most have her landing a beating for something petty.

"Blackwood!"

Looking up, I see Dave, who looks after ballistics and fingerprinting, standing across the room and holding two folders.

"Hey, man. How are you going?" Getting up, I go over and meet him halfway.

Dave is always swamped with work. Thankfully, though, we are good buddies, and he helps me out. Especially with this latest case of the serial killer plus our case is currently top priority. "Going good. Got those things for you that Pierce put a rush on. Gosh that guy can be annoying sometimes. It's like he comes to my office just to get a rise out of me."

"Me and you both, buddy. I mean he's decent enough, but damn, he does my head in sometimes."

Dave hands me one folder, and I take it. I open it up. I'm staring back at a familiar face, except she's younger. Elenore's younger face is right there in front of me, her beautiful blue eyes that hold so many secrets and still look the same. She wanted to protect herself, which is why the gun and diaries were hidden the way they were. She's been through something very traumatic and doesn't want to relive it. I can't blame her. If I'd suffered like she did, I'd want to forget as well.

"So what have you found out?" I ask Dave.

He stands beside me, with the folder open in front of me. Dave moves her picture aside, and we study the paperwork beneath it. "Well the only good set of fingerprints on the gun belong to Elenore. Also, the weapon has been shot before, as we established right away. The serial number had been filed off, but thanks to modern science, we've managed to get it to show up again. The owner of this gun was someone who has been murdered. He ran a corner store. The case is still unsolved."

My head flicks up, and I stare at him. "Are you sure?" I blurt out. *What did you do, Elenore?*

"As sure as there's sugar on my donut," he states matter-of-factly.

"Where's all this evidence taking us? This girl is like a box of secrets, just like the serial killer himself," I say. Dave nods his agreement. "Do you have the number for the unsolved case?"

Dave hands me the other larger folder he was holding. "Knew you'd want it. This one is pretty straightforward. Shop owner shot in a burglary. No credible witnesses, but there was this druggy who was sitting across the street, high as a kite. He told police that he saw a man and woman running from the scene. He mentioned that the man carried something large over his shoulder. He didn't get a good look, you know, he was high as a kite. There was also some video footage that was checked over."

I scan through the report quickly, and now I need to go to the evidence locker and pull out the evidence held there.

Elenore is like a Russian doll or Matryoshka doll. A doll inside a doll. Elenore... she's a secret within a secret. I need so many answers.

"Thanks, Dave. I'll look into it." Dave turns and leaves me to the million theories running through my mind. *What does all this mean?*

None of this tells me anything about my serial killer, but points me in another direction. I'm going to need to find some answers regarding Elenore's real parents, and find out who killed this shop owner.

Where do I start with it all?

I need to piece a timeline together of when these events happened and fill in the blanks.

I need you to hold on, Elenore. I know this is pulling me away from your case, but I need you to be strong in the meantime. Show your strength and don't let him win. Keep fighting. I beg her, knowing she can't hear me, but desperately somehow needing her to. Hold on. I'm coming for you.

I *will* find you.

CHAPTER FOURTEEN

Captor

ARRIVING AT THE HOUSE TONIGHT, the air is still, and the clouds have covered the stars in the sky. This evening would be a perfect night for a killing. If only I could bring myself to do it. My father would be so disappointed in me right now. It's a good thing he's dead and buried.

In his last days, our relationship was strained. We argued so much about the next choice of girl and the fact that I wanted to find my mother. I remember the fight we had a week before his death. It was then the seed of hostility was planted between us. It only kept growing until it turned into a large over grown weed.

Hate began fueling me, and with each death it kept me disconnected from anyone, until Elenore.

I walk toward the spot I took her — the kill spot. All my girls before her haven't lived past this point, each taking their last breath right here. Some gave a poor attempt to run — some didn't move because they had no strength left. Not her, though; she ran like her life depended on it. With each step she took toward that forest line, I'm sure hope fueled her, only to be snuffed out by me. With one single shot, she stumbled forward, her body crumbling, but she only gathered herself off the ground and didn't give up. Her fight and determination are compelling.

Reaching into my pocket, I pull out the first 'goodbye' letter she wrote and read it over again.

Dear Captor,

You've stolen me.

You've spilled my blood.

You've brought me pain.

But what you're yet to realize is… I'm a fighter.

I've been broken before.

I've at one point even lost the will to live.

So now you know… This information I gift to you.

I'm ready for you, so do your worst.

Sincerely,

Elenore

She was right. I did steal her. I have spilled her blood and brought her pain, but she's a fighter.

How was she broken before? Eventually the answer will reveal itself, that I'm sure of.

'*Do my worst,*' she said. Why can't I do that? I've spent years inflicting pain on these worthless girls, and now one comes along and twists my mind up with one single letter.

One damn letter.

That's all it took for me to gain some feelings and really think about what I was doing. I've read this note numerous times and always, always, it plays with my head. A part of me wants to let her go, but another part of me thinks I can't. I want to keep her for myself.

Could Elenore be the girl to melt away the ice which surrounds my heart and the hate which pulses through my blood?

Back in the house, I carry out my usual routine, checking the monitor to see if she's awake or asleep. Tonight, she's awake, sitting up against the wall near the food tray. My hands begin to tremble, and I'm not sure why. This is some kind of emotion I've never experienced.

This girl…

Shaking my head, I pull myself together and get a grip on whatever it is that's taking over.

Opening the door to the basement, I drag my mask over my face, pull my shoulders back and try to appear unfazed by her presence. I remind myself why I do this—hate, blood, pleasure in the pain, and my song of the night.

I've missed it.

Closing my eyes, I draw in a deep breath and release the mushiness that appears to be taking over and replace it with darkness.

My demeanor in this area changes; the world outside becomes forgotten. With each step down the stairs, a hardness claims me, devouring my insides like a tiger with its prey. The bars of her cell come into view, and I now have to prepare myself to see her in there. I don't hear her scurry like she did at the start. I step into view, and she lifts her head, her eyes meeting mine. My heart stops momentarily; her stare holds me in her trance.

"Good evening," she begins, a sweetness in her tone. Perhaps even a hidden agenda? I've come to learn with her that anything is possible. Hell, she pretended to be weak and unconscious in an attempt to escape.

I choose not to respond. Unlocking the food hatch, I reach in and grab the tray. I spy the note sitting neatly folded.

Elenore's hand reaches out and takes hold of my gloved one. I flinch back from her touch. I'm glad it wasn't skin to skin contact, even though that's what I desire. The touch of her lips pressed to mine stirs a hunger for so much more from her. I've touched her flesh, run my fingers over almost every part of her body as I inflicted pain on her. I know each of her curves, all of the scars that cover her body, and I know her sweet taste. I want more, so much more.

"Don't touch me," I growl, yet she still doesn't recoil.

I'd be lying if I said I didn't want to touch her more. But for appearance's sake, I keep up my facade.

My eyes bore into hers. A small smile plays on her lips. Her plump pink lips part slightly. She tilts her head back, exposing her neck invitingly. Quickly, I take the tray, locking the hatch again, and turning back toward the stairs.

My hands tremble with fury. Who does she think she is? I scrunch up the piece of paper with her beautifully handwritten note.

What do I see when I look in the mirror? Every single time I see the monster I've become. The darkness that's swallowed me whole.

When you're brought up on hate, it becomes a huge part of who you are. When Elenore looks at me she sees my darkness, and she senses my struggle with her. Yet, she holds steadfast to her promise of never giving up.

When my mother left, I had no one on my side to stand up for me, to stand up for what was right. My parents fought so much that he let her walk out, he didn't care for her. I recall Mom being so strong-willed and never backing down to my father. I only wish I had her strength of character. I've never seen or heard from her since she left. She could be dead for all I know, but no body has ever shown up.

I pace along the floorboards. All my thoughts are twisted in my head, and they keep replaying everything that's happened. Frustration pours through me, taking over. My hands slide along the bench knocking the tray, and all the utensils are sent clattering to the floor. *What is going on with me?*

Without realizing it, my feet move back toward the basement.

CHAPTER FIFTEEN

Elenore
Day Fourteen

HE'S ANGRY.

The steps along the floor above me pound for a moment. My letter must have hit home. I'm playing with a low-lit fire that could take ablaze at any moment. I don't know what came over me a moment ago. I have no idea why I grabbed him. When he looked at me, there was a softness in those usually black pools, and something stirred deep within me. An intense thrill shot right into me, and I desperately wanted to see his face, to touch his skin, for my lips to crush upon his once again.

Why is this exciting me? I desperately want to hate this man, my captor.

The footsteps pause, then a resounding clutter smashes against the floor above me, followed by a hammering of steps headed directly toward me. I don't move from my position; I don't want my captor to see how petrified I actually am. I'm facing his fury once again, only this time I'm better prepared. Perhaps he'll take me back out to the field and end it. I'm ready.

Sitting myself up taller, I keep my focus on him when he comes into view. There's a fire burning in those usually dead eyes.

"Are you all right?" I keep my voice at what I think is strong and neutral. I can't allow myself to show him weakness, not now. Even after being shot, tortured, and who knows what else is to come, I will never allow this man to witness me being weak. I was weak all those years ago but not anymore.

My father beat the weakness out of me. Every cut, bruise, and punch made me into who I am today. And just because my captor wants me to be afraid of him, I'll never show him the fear that wreaks havoc under my skin. I have a fire within me that spurs me on, pushes me to do better, and now it's driving me toward the man wearing down the cement floor with his pacing.

His breathing is erratic. Pausing, he glances my way. "You wanna know what I see when I look in the mirror?" he roars. So much venom pours off his tongue.

"I do." I press my body closer to the wall and support myself getting up. My leg still isn't the greatest, but the positive is my feet are feeling a little better today. They're still tender but it's becoming easier to stand on them again. With my heart lodged in my throat, I limp toward the bars. His hands grip them, and without thinking, I put mine over his, touching his gloves. Deep in the pit of my stomach, I have a strong desire to touch his skin. I slide my fingers up his arms, which are covered by a black leather jacket. At my touch, he doesn't flinch back like he did before. In fact, he closes his eyes and relishes the moment.

He has taped his sleeves closed as well as his mask which has a piece of tape running around his throat. It shows me that he's done this so many times before.

Hanging his head, he stares at the floor. His breathing has calmed a little. It's as though I'm baring all to him. I'm one hundred percent sure he's seen what's under this piece of cloth that covers me, and that thought actually excites me.

"What are you doing to me?" he whispers, his softer side making an appearance.

"It's not me. It's all you," I whisper so low as not to awaken the dragon lurking just under his skin.

My captor's head lifts, and his eyes bore into my own. "You should be dead." His rough voice mimics mine. This isn't the same person who's tortured me — well, at least, I don't think it is. The man beneath the mask holds a closet full of secrets of his own. Oh, how I would love to know them.

My hand slowly travels up his covered arms, my body now closer to the bars, which in turn means I'm closer to him. Still, he doesn't snap back.

"Why am I not dead?" I hesitantly ask. My trembling fingers reach his masked face. His eyes close briefly at my touch.

When they reopen, his focus stays on me. "Because I'm weak," he grits through his teeth. "You hold something over me, and I can't seem to bring myself to do it."

My heart leaps with joy at this news, not only for the fact that he can't do it, but also that he possibly holds some special place in his heart for me. "Then let me go, please?"

"I can't do that either." Slowly, he pulls away from me, turning toward the stairs, leaving me once again in this darkened cell which is now my own living hell.

A volcano erupts within me. "You can't keep me here! What am I going to be — your whore in a cage? Kill me, thanks. I'd rather death than being locked in this pathetic place for the remainder of my days," I scream at him through the bars.

I watch his head shake, before he turns back and races toward me. His hand pulls keys from the pocket of his black jeans.

Slowly, I take a step back from the bars. My whole body trembles, although I'm unsure what with — excitement or fear?

The keys rattle when my captor reefs the door open, stepping into my space. With only inches between us, I take a gamble and shuffle closer, my body flush with his. Raising his hand, he glides it down my cheek. Closing my eyes, I feel the emotion between us. The battle is only beginning, but who will win the war?

Dropping his fingers from my face, he begins removing the tape around his wrists, taking the gloves off. I watch fascinated. Dropping them to the floor, he takes my face in his bare hands, and my stomach twists into a million knots. He presses his masked face to mine, and I hear him inhale.

I cringe a little. It's been a while since I've showered and I'm sure I stink like death.

"I want to devour each and every part of you."

Bringing my arms up, I wrap them around his neck, pressing my body closer to him. I'm sure he can feel the pounding of my heart against his chest. This isn't what should be happening. I'm supposed to be fighting to get away from him. Perhaps this is how I survive, but a different kind of survival. I could become someone for him to care about, to confide in. Maybe I might be able to show him kindness.

"Do it," I find myself responding, so much longing in those two simple words.

One of his hands leaves my face, reaching behind him. Is he going to kill me instead?

When I spy the blade in his hand, I jump into fight mode. With everything I have in me, I shove him away. "No, don't you dare butter me up only to stick a knife in my back."

He steps toward me. I hold my hands up, limping backward.

"Do you think I'd do that?" he asks, with the blade still clutched in his hand.

I nod, fighting back the tears that threaten to flow. I can't allow this to be my final chapter, me charming the captor and him sticking a knife in my back.

"Even after I told you I couldn't bring myself to end your life?" he roars.

Startled, I continue to move back with each step he takes closer to me, descending on me as if I'm his prey. The fire's back in those eyes. I've awoken the dragon.

"How do I know what you're capable of?" I scream back. "You've kept me locked up here for I'm not sure how many days — they mold together now. You've beaten me, made me bleed. What do you think I'm going to do when you pull a knife out on me? Give my body to you willingly to slaughter?" I pant. My breath is ragged. Being so inactive and starved in this hell hole, even yelling has taken a toll on my health.

Turning away from me, I'm unable to see what

he's doing. All these ideas race through my head.

I could knee him in the groin, which would surely give me some time to get out and lock the door behind me. The keys are still in the door. This idea keeps dancing in my thoughts—I want to survive. I'll do anything I can.

He turns around, the knife now gone, I can't see it. I gasp, my hand coming to my mouth. He has cut a hole in his mask, revealing another part of him to me other than his eyes. "Why did you do that?" I ask, in shock.

Taking two large strides, he roughly takes my face in his hands again, only this time he presses his lips to mine.

My body ignites with newfound desire, wanting so much of this man who I know nothing about. *Why do my feelings betray me?* I could still escape.

All this bolts through my mind and is completely forgotten when he takes his mouth from mine, moving those same powerful kisses down my throat. I groan, craving the pleasure of his touch. I'm hungry for more.

My hands roam over his covered body. I wanted to touch him, his flesh, and have his body press against mine. His lips travel past my throat to my collarbone. Taking his masked face in my hands, I lift his head so my eyes can see his. The flame has gone, and pure lust fills those dark eyes. Although they aren't really black anymore—there's a shimmer of color to them, a greenish tinge mixes through them. I press my lips to his again, and he pulls me closer, as close as we can get.

"You taste so sweet," he growls against my lips.

Another groan leaves me.

The anger and fear that was pouring through me moments ago dissipates. If I were going to escape, this would be my chance.

CHAPTER SIXTEEN

Captor

I WANTED TO RIP HER dress from her delicate body. I wish I could reveal myself to her. I wonder what she would do.

Would she report me to the police? Or would she keep this a secret? She's such an enigma, a giant puzzle, and I need to know where all the pieces go before I reveal anything to her. Hungrily, I ravish her lips. My hands roam her thighs. Her skin is like silk—I can't resist. I want flesh to flesh with her, and it's every bit as good as what I thought it would be.

She hesitates briefly, and I wonder what's going through her head. It's as if I'm dipping my finger

in the honey pot, and its sweetness is so pleasurable that I want more. I can't get enough of her.

Her body shifts slightly. Lifting her up, I press her against the wall. The pressure I push against her with feels so right, yet so wrong.

What would my father think if he saw me fraternizing with the dirty, filthy girl?

Disappointment pours through my veins, as if an ice-cold bucket of water has been tipped over my horny body. I jump back, letting her fall to the floor.

"What the hell?" she curses. She gets up, and hurt shines through her pained eyes.

"I can't do this." My head is all over the place. I begin pacing — it's what I'm good at. Feeling like a failure, I turn to leave, but before I'm out the door I'm pounced on, being hit and scratched, even bitten.

"You vile, disgusting pig," she screams at me.

The hurt she must be feeling pours into every bite and scratch. I deserve it. I can't show her any more weakness. I pull her over my shoulder and allow her to fall to the concrete floor, hard.

Her stunned face looks up at me. "You're a pathetic excuse for a man."

Her words stab me right to the core. Anger takes over every fiber of my being. Pulling the blade from my pocket again, I press it against her neck. I need to remind her who's in charge, and it's not her.

"You're the filthy one here. You should be with the pigs. Unfortunately, I don't have any of those. I might invest, so I can feed your remains to them."

"You can't kill me, remember?" Even with a blade to her throat, she fights me.

"You'd be surprised what I can do." Moving the tip of the knife down her collarbone, I press harder. A drop of blood trickles out. Slowly, I move the blade. Her face pinches, and she begins breathing deeply, but though her eyes shimmer with tears they don't leave mine.

Guilt is a new emotion for me, yet looking at her, it wracks my entire body. The blade keeps moving. Now she has a gash from her collarbone right to the top of her breast.

It's such a relief for me — the need to inflict pain, to hold onto my father's traditions, and to keep my head in check.

This battle with myself is slowly becoming my greatest challenge, and also my greatest fear. Never have I ever experienced the type of emotions that are devouring me tonight. It's like it's not me. I've bedded girls before outside of this hell, and none of them have the effect on me that she does. She's a drug that I keep coming back for, again and again.

Elenore's sweet flavor sits on the tip of my tongue. I press my lips to hers, kind of like a final tasting before her demise. That's if I can manage it. Somehow, I need to work myself up to finishing her.

"Your time is coming," I manage to say through a nearly closed throat. Hell, it's hard speaking those words. Never have I choked on that sentence like this.

"Keep saying that." She hocks and spits at me, hitting me right in the eye.

I want to laugh, but I can't. Instead, I smack her with ferocity across her perfect face. Within seconds, a red welt appears, and it pleases me. "Be careful, precious. You never know the kind of hell coming your way."

CHAPTER SEVENTEEN

Roman

SITTING IN THE LARGE, OPEN office, I look out over the city. These people are made of money. Elenore's biological parents sit across from Pierce and me. When I told them we had news of their daughter, they told us to come right away.

"Mr. and Mrs. Billings, thank you for meeting with us so quickly," Pierce begins.

"Well, when you tell us it's about our lost daughter, of course we want answers," Elenore's mother says, desperation in her voice.

My focus is on her, drinking in her features. Characteristics like her dark hair and bright blue eyes scream Elenore. I looked into Elenore's eyes a fair bit before her kidnapping, and here before me is the spitting image of those exact eyes staring back at me.

Clearing my throat, I take over. "We are aware of the sensitivities of your daughter Rose's case. In our files, it states she was walking home from school. She stopped by a store, to get a sweet treat. As it turns out that shop was one that was robbed and the owner was killed on site. It's possible the people who killed them, took your daughter." I read this from the notes I've made.

Tears brim Elenore's mother's eyes. She nods, and her husband, Andrew, puts his arm around her for comfort. "She was such a strong, independent child. Rose desperately wanted to be like her friends and walk to school, so we let her, and after a few days our princess was gone." Tabatha's sobs echo in the large open space.

A lump forms in my throat, so I clear it away again. I take the picture of Elenore Suzie gave us from my folder, and slide it across to Mr. and Mrs. Billings. "This young woman has been taken by a possible serial killer. There was some blood left at the scene, and the results came back revealing it belongs to your daughter."

Tabatha picks up the photo and studies it. Her hand flies to her mouth. Tears stream down her face. "It's her. I remember those rosy pink cheeks—that's how we named her. She's had them since birth."

Andrew takes the photo, and we're met with the same shocked reaction. "So, she's alive?" Andrew asks. Tears stream down his face. He has dark hair as well, but unlike Elenore, he has dark brown eyes. I have no doubt that this man didn't get to where he was by his wits alone; he's obviously fought for what he wants. Hopefully, Elenore inherited that trait, and it could mean all the difference for her.

Pierce takes over. He knows that talking about this is challenging for me. I wish I could find her, save her from the monster. "Yes, she was, but now... we're unsure. Usually, with this serial killer, we've found the bodies of his victims within seven days of their disappearance. Only your daughter hasn't shown up."

Tabatha and Andrew turn and look at each other. I can see the fear in their faces; I had that look myself when I discovered she was gone.

"Wha-what do we need to do? Do we need to offer up a reward?" Tabatha asks.

"No, I don't think it would be wise for him to be aware of whose daughter he has hostage," Pierce quickly responds.

I have to agree with him. Of course, this killer doesn't realize who he's got. He obviously assumes Elenore is just another girl.

"I can't just sit by and wait to see if her body shows up! We've missed out on her life for the past fourteen years, and now she's missing again. Where has she been?" Tabatha asks, releasing a heavy sign, her frustration evident.

"Well, she goes by Elenore Burrows now. Her apparent parents, who we now assume were kidnappers, disappeared, and she was left alone at seventeen. She was adopted by her neighbor. From what her adopted mother has told us, she was treated extremely poorly prior to her adoption," I say.

"But why did no one recognize her? Why didn't they call the police?" Tabatha continues. I can't blame her for the anger in her tone. I would be the same as her, wanting all the answers. Since reading Elenore's diaries my blood has boiled with so much madness. I want to catch her parents and make them pay.

"They altered her appearance, cutting her hair, and when her neighbor did call the police they kept Elenore hidden so the officers wouldn't suspect anything. This is what we're going off from reports we've read."

Andrew stands from his seat and paces the cream carpeted floor. "Well, what can we do?" he asks. "We want to help."

Pierce interjects. "Mr. and Mrs. Billings, we understand the hurt and confusion you must be experiencing right now. We're doing everything we can to find your daughter, and we're also searching for the people who took her in the first place."

Tabatha nods while dabbing a tissue at her now blotchy face.

"The people who took her must have taken her as she was in the wrong place, wrong time," I say. Both the Billings' faces mirror each other's as the shock of what we've told them begins to sink in.

"It was so long ago—I remember giving her some money because she had finished all her homework and I wanted to reward her with a treat," Mr. Billings says from his standing position. I nod.

"We understand this situation is hard. We're so sorry this has happened. We will keep you informed with what's going on in the cases as we're able to," Pierce answers.

"Cases?" Tabatha asks a puzzled look comes across her face.

"Yes. There's another case we are investigating that's connected to a piece of evidence we found in your daughter's possession." I choose not to let them in on the information regarding the gun. Less information is best at this time, regarding how their daughter was brought up.

Back at the office, Pierce and I are going through our notes. Pierce hasn't read the diaries, and I'm not sure he wants to because he hasn't asked. I've given him a run down on things I've read so far.

Also keeping a few things to myself.

"I'm going to watch this video on the shooting," I announce, as I get up and go to the TV and set about getting it ready to watch. I know this isn't our case, but the captain has allowed us to look over both since we're already handling Elenore's case.

"Good idea. We need all the answers we can get. I'm assuming we won't get much from it if it didn't provide any clues to the officers who were in charge of the investigation previously."

I know he is right, but I need to check anything and everything possible. The most insignificant details might give us a clue. I know all of this doesn't give me much or anything to work on as to where Elenore is now, but we need to find the people who abducted her from her home in the first place so we can rule them out as her kidnappers now.

"Yeah, I know, but I need answers. Even if it holds nothing, at least I've checked. I also want to track down that witness who was apparently across the road at the time. That's if he's still alive." I'm not holding much hope; let's face it, he was a drug user.

As predicted, the video gives us nothing. There are blurry images of a man and woman; they try to rob the shop owner and when he stands up for himself, pulling out his gun, they raise their hands in defeat. Everything pauses on the screen before the man leaps and begins struggling with the owner and then, kills him. Moments after the killing, they walk out, then return leaving with a lump of something over their shoulders. Elenore?

I look up from my computer screen. Pierce is gone again. Turning to an officer standing near me, I ask, "Did you see where Pierce went?"

He shrugs, shaking his head. "Nah man, he just hopped up and was gone." He rises from his seat shrugging, then walks away. Picking up my phone, I hit Pierce's name, and he answers after the first ring.

"Where are you?" I bark.

"Tracking down the drug addict you mentioned."

Well, at least he's doing something helpful, but I don't understand why he didn't tell me. I want to get to the bottom of this extremely messy puzzle. Leaning back in my seat, I take the journal I'd been reading and pick up where I left off.

Dear Diary,

Another day in the black room. I do try really hard to stay in my parents' good books, but I fail all the time. Today's reason was I didn't get all of my daily chores done by lunchtime. Well, how could I when they wanted me to take every weed out of the garden and plant a new garden, then do laundry, dishes— basically clean the house from top to bottom?

Of course, I have no hope of succeeding. And again, I haven't had a chance to stash my supplies back in here, they've kept me in here that much and been hanging around home so much more. I haven't been able to sneak down and stock up.

I can't keep going like this. My father is becoming more violent.

One day, I'll have the strength to do what I need to.

One good thing that happened yesterday was I got to hang out with Dean again. We meet in the library on a regular basis and talk books and school. He shows me what's being worked on at school so I can keep up with my learning. He's turned out to be a great friend. He's hinted that he likes me, but I don't think I want to be in a relationship with him. I'm not ready for that.

My father has turned me off men. I wish I understood why they treated me like they do. Dean offered to take me to the hospital, but I declined because I'd be in more trouble if I came home with my arm bandaged up. They want me to suffer — they enjoy seeing my pain.

I've read so many books lately about people who have come away from this kind of violence and have led great lives. They become amazing people and don't let their past affect them.

I want to be like that.

How do I escape though? What if I ran away

and they found me, I'd surely be dead.
One day, my chance will come.
Love,
Elle

Who's this Dean? He's shown up a lot in these last few entries. Perhaps he could provide me with some answers as to where her original kidnappers are.

Holding the notebook in my hands, I glance over Elenore's teenage handwriting. This is the last journal. I want to know her story even if it's like reading a nightmare.

CHAPTER EIGHTEEN

Elenore

I LIE ON MY BED, waiting for death to take me. My body trembles, shivering with a fever. It's been what feels like days since my captor has come back. I haven't been fed since the day he left when he gave me one tray of bread and water along with a pen and paper. The showers come on occasionally. We're back to square one.

I'm not sure what he wants me to do with the pen and paper. I don't think I've even got the strength to lift the pencil—that's how long it feels like since I've been fed properly. Now I've come down with what feels like the cold from the devil himself.

He has blackened my room from the outside. The little bit of sunlight that once shone in is now covered. Even the little light that's usually on in my cell flickers on and off, and when it's off I'm met with an eerie blackness that makes this situation like something from a horror movie. All I'm waiting for is to be slaughtered, carved into a million little pieces and scattered over the earth, with no one none the wiser as to what's become of me. With the captor, who knows what he's capable of doing.

I wonder if Roman is still looking for me. When I close my eyes at night, it's him and Suzie that appear in my dreams. Only then they're invaded by the lady in the rose garden. I've had that dream about five times now, but nothing new is shown to me — just the lady and little girl playing. I wish it would reveal more to me, but then my captor's flaming red eyes take over and I startle awake.

My fight has taken a whopper of a punch since my captor came to my cell last and teased me. I should have done the knee-in-the-groin thing, I could either be free or dead now. I can't give up though — it's not me; it's not who I am.

With what strength I have, I pull the pen and paper from under my bedding. Sitting up slowly, I put pen to paper.

Dear Captor,

Do you find pleasure in my tortured screams?

My darkened cell is my own living nightmare.

Why do you continue to play this game? Why don't you just kill me?

You've almost broken me all over again — but I've held firm. I've pushed through the pain you've inflicted. And now I'm seeing a side of you I never knew could exist. A side I connect with. A side I could grow to like.

Your touch on my skin… it ignites a fire within.

Only time will tell what will come of it.

With love,

Elenore

The words read true. These aren't my deepest secrets, I keep those locked away from the world so people in my life don't see the ugly in me.

CHAPTER NINETEEN

Captor

Day Eighteen

IT'S BEEN FOUR DAYS SINCE I've been back. I wonder if she's dropped dead yet. A small, very small part of me hopes that she has, because it will mean I don't have to do it. Yes, weak, I know. I think I need to kill again to work myself up to removing the biggest hassle I've ever faced. Guilt has been wracking me. How did I let things get to where they did the other night? Her soft blue eyes always swallow me up and make me feel things I shouldn't.

Inside the house, it's quiet. I look at the monitor. She lies still, unmoving. I catch a glimpse of something sitting on the tray I left there days ago. *Another note.* It's neatly folded and resting in the middle of the tray, as if it's waiting for me. I wonder if it's another insult which stirs me up, but then I want to get close to her. Why can't I be stronger?

She begins coughing, as though one of her lungs is trying to escape out of her throat. *She's sick...*

Knowing this does something to me. Do I want to help her or not? With remorse getting the better of me, I pull out another tray. Placing another pen and paper neatly on there for her to use, I then turn and heat up some soup from a can. Then I place bread and a bottle of water on the tray. I leave it there while I retrieve the old one and see what she's written.

When I'm down there, she faces the wall with her back to me. Not acknowledging me at all. It's like a stab to the stomach. I've hurt her. I didn't want to, and I still don't. What am I going to do?

Once back upstairs, I check the monitor again. She looks over her shoulder, then goes back to the same position she was in. My hands tremble as I open the letter. The writing is so messy compared to her first one. She's weak. I've starved her for the last few days and punished her with the cold shower going on and off. There's also been a chill in the air which explains why she's sick. I hear her coughing once again, and it pulls at my heartstrings. If only my heart wasn't ice. Although since she's come into my life, it's ever-so-slowly beginning to thaw.

A lump forms in my throat as I read her words. What she describes in this letter — the fire within — I feel it as well. I have from the moment she put up such a brave fight to survive. We have something in common, this dark emotion, and I wonder if that's there is to it. If that's all we share.

I grab a pen and paper and begin writing a return note.

Dear Elenore,

Your screams were once a song in the night that I craved.

You're a fighter, and I appreciate that. You amaze me.

I'm evil, even if I don't want to be. My life is full of death. This is what I need to do to survive the guilt I feel every day you live.

The desire to kill isn't as strong as what it once was. That's because of you. You are something new to me, and I like it a lot. But I can never allow my feelings to get the better of me.

Let's make a deal. I'll tell you about me if you tell me more about you?

With love,

Your captor

After folding the letter, I place it on the tray. Going to the medicine cupboard, I retrieve what she needs to fight the cold she's come down with because of me.

What am I going to do? I can't keep her here for much longer. She needs to go. To either be found dead, or escape.

I'm not ready to let her go, though.

CHAPTER TWENTY

Elenore
Day Nineteen

HE CAME BACK. I DIDN'T want to talk to him or even acknowledge him. Thankfully, he left me some food and medication. I'm feeling more human today, but can one really be human if they're locked up like an animal? He's also removed the cover over my window; now, the sunlight shines through again. I miss being outside. I want to be in the fresh air, to actually witness the birds singing in the bright green trees. Hell, to have a bath would be fantastic.

The letter he wrote me was somewhat touching, for a damn killer. I need to reply in case he comes back tonight.

Taking the writing equipment, I set myself up to write back to my captor.

Dear Captor,

Yes, I'm a fighter. I grew up in a home where I was the punching bag and the cutting board for my parents. No person, at the age I was, should have to go through that much pain. The pain you inflict on me, though, is another version. When you impose it on me now, it hurts more because I thought that something had possibly switched between us. Where do I stand with you? Will you ever let me go?

Why do you do what you do? I've never heard of this type of barbaric torture before. Don't you have a family? A mom, dad, or anything... brothers and sisters? Me, I have no one except Suzie, my adoptive mother. She is truly amazing, and it saddens me that you're keeping me from her.

Please, if you have a heart, then let me go.

You want secrets? I have a few. But one I think might interest you, but you'll have to do what I tell you. Go to my old family home. There you'll find something about me that no one knows. That home holds my secret. Go figure it out.

With love,

Elenore

Roman

I FOUND DEAN. HE WASN'T too keen to talk to me when I rang him, but I pushed, even to the point when I was ready to drag his ass down to the station and lock him up, just to scare him. He knows something, but I'm not sure what, although I intend to find out.

Standing outside his large workplace, I wait for him to leave. I plan to talk to him when he's on his lunch break.

"You Detective Blackwood?" The voice behind startles me. Spinning around, I'm met with a big, burly guy with the voice of a teenager. He has tattoos up each arm and around his neck. Wow! Not what I'd pictured. "What are you looking at?"

"Sorry… Yes I'm detective Blackwood, Roman." I clear my throat, I extend my hand, he takes it giving a strong handshake. "I'm Dean."

"I need some information on your old friend Elenore." The color drains from his face. He starts fidgeting with his shirt and buttons. Is he hiding something?

I step into his space. He tries to shuffle back. My hand lashes out, gripping the collar of his white button-up shirt. "Tell me what you know."

Pushing my hand off him, he shuffles on his feet as he stutters to find the right words. "L-look, I've tried to p-put this behind me, and it's n-not something I want t-to relive."

"What is it?" I yell, becoming frustrated with his dance-around. "She's missing and I need information," I grit out between my teeth.

As burly as he looks, I think he may actually wet himself with nerves. "You need to go to her old house… d-down in the basement. There's a reason that house didn't sell until this year, because Elenore didn't want it s-sold until she was ready."

What is this guy on about?

"What? So I need to go to her old house and look for what, exactly?"

"You'll kn-know it when you f-find it."

I want to shake the guy, shake some damn sense into him. Maybe she writes about what happened at the house in her journals? *Those last few entries?*

"Thanks." Without another word, I leave, racing back to the office.

I need the end of her books to give me a clearer picture and perhaps the answers I'm seeking. I can't enter her old home unless we have probable cause. I have to find some first.

CHAPTER TWENTY-ONE

Captor
Day Nineteen

I WONDER IF ELENORE WILL share her secrets with me. I want her to tell me all of them.

Arriving back at the familiar house, a thought comes. *What am I going to do if I let her go?* Court her? Make her fall in love with the other me? That shouldn't be hard. Ladies love me—I've never gone without a woman when I needed one.

Inside, I hear coughing... She's still sick. I check the monitor. She's awake. I'm not sure if I'm prepared to face her after what's happened. She's like a temptress who I want to devour, but I can't.

I gather a tray together, fill it with food, and this time I add a small chocolate bar I picked up today, and again I head down to the basement.

She's up waiting. Her eyes are firmly trained on me. Elenore sits against the far wall, as far away from me as she can be. I don't blame her.

"Finally decided to show your face." There's no kindness in her words.

"You ignored me last time." I squat down to her level.

Pink flushes her cheeks. *Yes, pretty girl, I saw.* "So you're watching me?"

"I'm always watching." I unlock the latch, and she has another coughing fit. I fight with myself, but I don't go in there and try to help her. If I do that, I know I'll most likely end up with her in my arms and me relishing her touch once again. I can't do that. "Are you all right?" I'm genuinely concerned for her health, and I notice that she's been taking the medicine I left, the bottle appears to be half empty. Thankfully, I've purchased more.

After she finishes her fit, she replies, her voice raspy. "I'm fine. What do you care? Do what you have to do. You know, *family traditions,* and all."

Ouch! That stings.

I stand to leave her once again. I wish I could let her go, but things are becoming more and more challenging.

Back upstairs, again, I unfold her letter, and I'm left speechless. Now I've got to find out what she means regarding her old house. Before I get back to work, I pen another letter to her.

Dear Elenore,

I was a punching bag also. My family tradition is something I now wouldn't wish on anyone else. If I ever have any.

I did have a mother, and she left me in the hands of a monster. For that indiscretion, she became dead to me.

I killed that monster, and it was the best kill I've ever done.

With love,

Your captor

I've never told anyone that secret. I wonder if that will change her perspective of me. It couldn't be any worse than what's already in her head.

Folding the page up, I put it on the tray with some soup, medicine, water, and a chocolate bar.

She's thawing my heart so much faster now. I wonder what her secret is.

Roman

BACK ON SUZIE'S STREET, THE sun beats down on us. I raced over here once I read what she'd written as her last entry. I had to skim through all the other pages first to make sure I didn't miss anything.

Suzie stands beside me, clasping a tissue, dabbing at her red-framed eyes. Someone else lives here now, and I'm not sure how they will react. I've placed a call to my supervisor, and he's sending over a team. I've rung Pierce and left a voice message for him as well, so hopefully, he shows up soon.

"Are you sure that's what she meant?" Suzie's voice shakes with emotion. She really didn't know Elenore's darkest secrets. I'm confident I know them all now. I hold out the last journal to Suzie, open at the closing entry. She takes it from my hands and starts to read, sobs take over.

Dear Diary,

Today it all ended. My parents are no more, and I'm free. It feels good.

Love,

Elle

CHAPTER TWENTY-TWO

Elenore
Day Twenty

Nighttime has come around again, and he hasn't come back yet. His last letter opened more of him for me. Again, I've written a reply, and I can only hope that he softens. I've seen a glimmer of what appears to be happiness in him, then it changes. He's broken, like me. His father was a monster, and he killed him.

Seems we have something in common.

Something upstairs startles me. It doesn't sound familiar, though. I can usually pick if it's my captor — not that it's ever anyone else. But his steps are generally heavier.

Footsteps hit the stairs to the basement. Standing up, I move to the back of the cell. *Something's wrong.* I wrap my arms around my waist and wait for whoever it is to appear.

I don't have to wait long before a masked face appears, only this person isn't my captor. This is an intruder, who knows about my captor and what he does. He's taller and slinkier than my captor. This man doesn't look as if he's here for anything other than trouble. I have nowhere to run or hide. I'm trapped like an animal.

"Well, well, well, look who we have here. I should've known."

He has a different voice; he isn't my captor.

Panic sets in. I begin looking around for something to use as a weapon. The only thing that would even offer any kind of help is the metal tray. As quick as I can, I race the few steps to retrieve it, and move back to my corner.

Does he have keys? I scan his body and notice none, but it doesn't mean they aren't in his pockets. He's dressed all in black, like my captor, with tape around his wrists, neck, and even his ankles.

"Who are you?" I ask with whatever strength I can muster.

"Your worst nightmare." His hand reaches into his pocket, and I hear the jangle of keys.

My heart hammers in my chest. Now I'm sure I'm going to die. I have nothing, and my captor isn't here to help me.

As he unlocks the door, I watch him, focusing everything I have on this intruder. I must look like a scared mouse. His mask is different from my captor's because he already has a hole in it for his mouth, whereas my captor only has his eyes showing. I've learned to read my captor's eyes extremely well, and this intruder's eyes tell me he's here for blood.

The door creaks loudly as he opens it, stepping into my space. I'm ready to fight; I won't go down without one. The one night I wish for my captor to be here, and he's not. I need him.

"He's going to pay for what he's done. You'll suffer for his past." Speaking those last words, he lunges at me. I use as much force as I can and slam the tray down, connecting it with his shoulder. He cries out but I don't stop. I swing the tray, left, right, up and down, with as much force as I can muster. Every which way possible, I continue to smash it into him. As I do so, I move around my cell toward the open door. I'm almost out when he bends down low, and head butts me right in the stomach. I fall to the floor, winded.

"You're a feisty one. I can see why he kept you. Now you bleed." Throwing me over his shoulder, he takes me to the room I haven't been in for a while. I'm frightened of what this man will do to me. He's so much darker than my captor; his eyes tell me that he's out for blood, and he's not leaving until he gets it.

He drops my body on the gurney. I try getting up and running. I fail. With a closed fist, he punches me directly in the cheek. Tears fall and pool in my ears. I don't want to show weakness to this man, but he's already going to inflict pain that I know I may not survive.

My eyes follow his every movement. He searches drawers until he finds what he's seeking. Turning around, he greets me with a smirk, one that you can tell isn't the good kind. In his hand is a blade, like the one my captor used on me when I first arrived here. A pocket knife of some sort.

"Because of what he hasn't done yet, he needs to be taught a lesson. You ready to bleed?"

Swallowing hard, I let my focus stay on him.

He pauses a moment. "You a fighter, little girl?"

I say nothing.

He presses the blade into the cut already on my collarbone. "I see he's tried and failed, like we knew he would one day."

We? What is this lunatic on about?

"You'll pay for this," I threaten. I know that my captor and I have a love/hate relationship, but he wouldn't want this to happen to me.

"We'll see about that. You might be dead so it won't matter." His voice holds promise. His evil smirk is back as the blade digs deeper into my flesh. I scrunch up my face and pray for this to end soon. It doesn't, though.

With the blade, he cuts open the cloth covering my body exposing me in my undies and bra. I close my eyes and wish to be taken to my happy dream where the little girl with the roses are, and to her mother. Images flicker through my head—Roman, Suzie, the little girl, roses, her mother—over and over in my mind.

A burning sensation builds in my stomach. A scream erupts from me, and I can't stop. I feel his hands move over my body, leaving new cuts in their wake. Fuzziness fills my head, and I will for it to take over quickly so I don't have to endure this excruciating pain.

Opening my eyes, my stomach is covered in blood, and I don't see the intruder anywhere.

He's gone.

Left me.

Blood pours from me. I don't have the strength to even attempt getting up as bright spots appear in my vision.

Please, take me. I can't deal with this anymore.

Blackness takes over.

To Be
Continued…

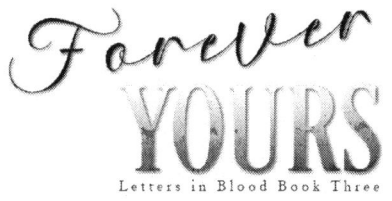

Letters in Blood Book Three

LIZ LOVELOCK

Dear Captor,

You show me you care, but then something changes. The brightness in your eyes shines through on your good days, but when you come to me on your dark days, the blackness has taken over.

At least I know what I'm in for . . . pain.

You've managed to crawl under my skin in the most excruciating yet sensual way, my darkest secrets are now yours, and the emotions I feel for you are something I've never felt before. This sensation is strange, yet exhilarating.

Do you feel the same?

If you do love me, please . . . let me go.

Forever yours,

Elenore

Forever Yours

Letters in Blood Book Three

available 15 November 2017

ALSO BY LIZ LOVELOCK

Lost Series
The Lost One
The Missing One

Unforgiven Series
Dangerous Love
Forbidden Love *(coming soon)*

Canyon Bay Series
Someday

Letters in Blood series
Dear Captor

To keep up with upcoming releases and news visit me at my

Website
www.lizlovelockauthor.com

Facebook
www.facebook.com/authorlizlovelock

Twitter
www.twitter.com/LizLovelock

Goodreads
www.goodreads.com/author/show/8268717.Liz
_Lovelock

Instagram
www.instagram.com/lizlovelock/

Email
lizlovelockauthor@gmail.com

ABOUT LIZ LOVELOCK

I'm a wife, mother, reader, blogger, and now an author. I'm always busy doing something as I have so much going on, and my three little ones keep me on my toes.

I'm from bright and sunny Queensland, Australia. I have always been a reader. When I was little, I would be up late reading *Garfield* and *Asterix* comic books and also *Footrot Flats*. When I hit high school, they gave us *Tomorrow When the War Began* by John Marsden, and from there my love of books continued to grow.

I keep a notebook and pen beside my bed for when those late-night ideas pop into my head, plus I'm a stationery addict and love pens, notebooks, and, well, anything stationery.

ACKNOWLEDGEMENTS

I'll say sorry first in case I miss anyone. I'd like to thank my editors, Kaylene Osborne from Swish Design and Editing, and Lauren Clarke from Lauren Clarke Editing. Without you girls, I'd be thoroughly lost; you've pushed me with this one as well. Thanks for all your advice and guidance and for putting up with my timing problems.

Thank you Virginia Tesi Carey for fitting me in on short notice and polishing up my work to make it squeaky clean. You're awesome!

Special thanks to Tami from Integrity Formatting for helping make my work look beautiful. You do such an amazing job.

To my fantastic team of betas: Amanda, Rachel, and Melissa your input is so valuable. Thank you for all your feedback—you're all amazing. And thanks for being patient with me and pushing me to do better.

A huge thank you to Marisa-Rose from Cover Me Darling for designing another perfect cover, and working with me until I was happy. It is everything I wanted it to be. I love it!

Thank you to Give Me Books for your help with the release. A MASSIVE thank you to all blogs who participated in the release, and to everyone who shared anything, I truly appreciate it. We authors would be lost without your assistance.

These next mentions are my other halves of the author world. Without their constant support and pushing, I may have given up a long time ago. They're my cyber sisters spread far and wide around Australia and America, so thank you to Jemma Brown aka JB Heller, Stephanie Smith, Emma Fitzgerald, Felicia Tatum, and Belle Brooks. These ladies are truly amazing. I'd be lost without our chats.

To Anastasia, your help has been truly amazing. Without you and your input I'd be all over the place.

To my Flock, I love you, girls. Your support is truly nothing short of amazing. I know I have a safe place in my group with you all. Thank you.

And to my readers, I feel blessed to have your continuous support. Thank you.

To my family, my husband, you're truly wonderful. You've never given up on me. You sit and listen when I need to vent out my frustrations, never once complaining about it. I love you. To my three beautiful children, Millie, Cale, and Finn, you all test my patience, but I'm so grateful to have you in my life to love. Families are forever.

Printed in Great Britain
by Amazon